*Silent Prejudice* is a work of fiction. Names, characters, places, and incidents are the products of the author's imagination or are used fictitiously. Any resemblance to actual events, locales, or persons, living or dead, is entirely coincidental.

Copyright © 2021 Jill Ramsower

All rights reserved. In accordance with the U.S. Copyright Act of 1976, the scanning, uploading, and electronic sharing of any part of this book without the permission of the publisher is unlawful piracy and theft of the author's intellectual property. Thank you for your support of the author's rights.

Print Edition ISBN: 9781734417289

Cover Model: Holly Ardron
Photographer: Nicole Jopek

❦ Created with Vellum

## Books by Jill Ramsower

### The Savage Pride Duet
Savage Pride
Silent Prejudice

### The Five Families Series
Forever Lies
Never Truth
Blood Always
Where Loyalties Lie
Impossible Odds
Absolute Silence
Perfect Enemies

### The Fae Games Series
Shadow Play
Twilight Siege
Shades of Betrayal
Born of Nothing
Midnight's End

*To Rah Rah:*
*There's no one I'd rather tease, argue, or debate with because every word between us is spoken from a place of love. Romance can be fleeting, but soulsisters are forever.*

# CHAPTER 1

"What the hell happened?" Nevio asks between heaving breaths. "I thought I'd catch up and see why you were running off, but you were like a thing possessed."

*You should have let me run.*

I want to scream at him. Take out all my frustrations and anger on him for imposing on my moment of crisis. He would be an easy target. The man who has no idea he's my brother.

*None of this is his fault.*

It's true. He doesn't deserve my wrath. He was only trying to help by coming after me, and lashing out would only make me feel worse.

I close my eyes and inhale a slow, long breath, keeping my jaw wired shut.

Nevio bends at the waist and leans his hands on his knees to steady his breathing. "My first thought was that my brother said something to upset you, but then I remembered he left for the city early this morning. Was it your mom? You gotta tell me what happened, Isa. I can tell you're upset."

His instinct is accurate, but not in the way he might imagine. Zeno wasn't heartless or condescending.

He told me the truth for once.

A truth that's even harder to swallow than the years of muttered slights. So hard that I felt no choice but to run from that truth. Literally. I raced from Hardwick with no destination in mind and now find myself exhausted with a twisted ankle, collapsed into a hopeless heap on the shore of Tuxedo Lake. I would happily wallow in pain if I were alone, but that's not the case. Nevio chased me down, and I had to give him some semblance of an explanation.

I study the man standing fifteen feet away and try to wrap my brain around the knowledge that he is my brother. My half brother. I think of our kiss and the handful of daydreams I'd entertained when I'd considered having a relationship with him—a sexual relationship—and my stomach convulses violently. This time, I can't keep it held in. I lean to the side and throw up my breakfast. Thankfully, I didn't eat much, but it's all there.

Nevio starts to rush over. I frantically wave him off, desperate for him to stay away. Having him close will just make the nausea worse. There'd been no way for me to know that Nevio was my half brother, but it doesn't lessen my disgust when I consider where things might have gone between us. It's too grotesque to consider. I shut those thoughts securely into a concrete vault where they can never see the light of day again.

"I'm fine. I'm fine." I wipe at my mouth with the back of my hand. "Guess I ran a little too much right after eating."

He takes one more step closer. I keep my eyes locked on his feet, avoiding his questioning gaze and the sight of my father's sad eyes.

"Isa, you're scaring me here. What the hell is going on?"

Tears stream from my eyes like rain down a windshield. I can't fathom where it's all coming from, but there's no end in sight.

Nevio's kindness and distress make it all so much harder because, on top of everything else, a part of me grieves for the loss of a brother I never knew I had. So many years down the drain when we could have been such close friends. Had we known, we would never have lost touch. I feel it with a certainty deep in my bones. That unique bond formed between siblings would have kept us close, but that opportunity was robbed from us. Not only did we miss out on years of connection, but I may never know Nevio as a brother. Zeno confessed the truth in his letter, but he also begged me to keep Nevio's paternity a secret.

Can I honor such a burdensome request?

I'm not the only person to consider when trying to answer that question. No matter how aggrieved I may feel, my injuries are fractional compared to Nevio's. He is the most obvious victim of this charade between our families, and he has no idea. I firmly believe he deserves to know the truth. But who am I to divulge such a secret? I can disagree all I want with Elena's choice to keep her affair a secret, but that doesn't give me the right to come between mother and son. I certainly shouldn't go off half-cocked in a fit of my own raging emotions and rip his world to shreds. This is not the time or place. I have to keep my mouth shut, no matter what it costs me, at least for now.

"It was my mom," I blurt. "You know how she gets under my skin. And it's even worse now that I'm older."

"Whatever she did must have been pretty bad, considering we're halfway around the lake and your tears are still falling." He's not sure he believes me, and his suspicion is reasonable. I've never been an emotional person, so I can only imagine how shocked he must have been to see me bolt for the trees.

I have to find a way to explain away my actions. If I don't, he'll become suspicious.

While I hadn't wanted anyone outside our family to know about my mother's gambling problem, telling Nevio was my best way out of this situation. It's the one thing I can give him that could genuinely justify my outburst of emotion, so I take a deep breath and surrender a secret of my own.

"I decided to stay with my parents instead of going back to the city and finishing school because I discovered that my mother got into financial trouble. She has developed a problem with gambling that I wasn't aware of until I came home. I didn't tell you or anyone else because the bookie she owed was a Giordano family bookie, and I was worried my father's name would be smeared by her actions. I paid off her debt, and it's all over now, but putting my life on hold to rebuild my college savings has been hard on me. I was almost done with school, and now I won't be able to finish for another year. I lost the new apartment I was going to move into and had to quit my job so I could stay with my parents and save. It's been a difficult couple of weeks. Mom said something insensitive this morning, and it set me off. All the emotions hit me at once, and I had to get out of there. And with my shit luck, I twisted my ankle right before you caught up with me." I rub at the offending appendage, which has begun to swell, though the pain has eased to a dull throb. "That's why I was so upset."

"Shit, Isa." He hurries over to inspect the injury. "You should have told me about your mom. I could have helped."

I breathe deeply with relief at successfully dodging further interrogation but stiffen at his nearness. "I didn't need help."

"Maybe, but there's also no reason for you to deal with something like that alone. You know I'd keep a secret for you. Hell, there's plenty I don't tell my family." He gingerly lifts my ankle and rolls the joint in a small circle. "It's definitely sprained, but I don't think anything's broken."

"Yeah, it's already starting to feel better."

Nevio peers back in the direction we came with a frown. "That may be, but there's no way you're walking all the way home on it." Nodding to himself, he slips an arm beneath my knees and tries to scoop me up in a bridal carry, but I screech and flail.

"What the hell are you doing?" My response is a gross overreaction, but it can't be helped. I'm petrified of him thinking there's something between us or doing anything that he might interpret as encouragement.

He releases me to my feet and gapes at me as though I've gone batshit crazy. "I *was* going to carry you to the road, but I suppose you can walk in pain if you'd prefer that to being near me."

"No! It's not that. I just…" *God*, how do I explain this? "You just surprised me." I hold out my arm to urge him closer. "If you'll let me lean on you, that should be plenty of support."

Doubt twists his lips, but he returns to my side. "I figured someone could bring a car around to pick us up from there."

I nod and slide my left hand around to cup his shoulder from behind, using his solid mass as a crutch. His right arm supports me from behind, keeping me pressed against his side. We take a few steps to test our system, and I minimize my hobbling so that he doesn't insist on carrying me.

"My mom could probably come pick us up," he offers while we ease over the uneven terrain. "But if you'd rather try to get ahold of someone from your house, we can do that instead."

"No, your mom would be great if she's available." I need to be alone to process everything, and that'll never happen if my family gets wind of my panicked flight. The questions would be endless.

We make it to the road in less time than I expect. I

suppose I'm owed at least one shred of good fortune in the midst of my nuclear meltdown of a life.

Elena brings the car around and studies me with curious eyes but doesn't pry for answers. She drives me to my parents' cottage and agrees to tell my mom that I went home with a headache. They will be far less curious about me going home sick than if they knew I'd twisted my ankle after freaking out and sprinting down to the lake. Yet again, Elena is my saving grace. A beacon of kindness and understanding piercing the darkness. I may not agree with her choices in life, but I find it hard to fault her. Each of her thoughts and deeds is motivated by the purest of intentions.

I offer her a genuine thanks before allowing Nevio to help me to the cottage door.

"You need me to get you set up inside? I can put together an ice pack and grab you some ibuprofen."

I smile and make sure to leave a buffer of space between us. "Thank you, Nev, but I'm really okay."

He lifts his chin and peers down at me skeptically. "If you say so. Make sure to rest, and we can talk more about your mom later. Don't think I'm letting that slide." He leans in before I can stop him and drops a kiss on my forehead. "Text me if you need anything."

The touch of his lips on my skin is like a scarlet letter condemning me. A brother's kiss isn't necessarily inappropriate, but in this instance, anything at all between us is too much because he doesn't know. He doesn't intend his touch in a brotherly fashion, and it makes my skin crawl.

He glides down the front steps without a clue.

My eyes seek out Elena, who watches us from the car. Her face is inscrutable, keeping me in the dark about what she might think of Nevio's affection toward me.

Does it bother her to see us together? Would she consider telling Nevio about her affair in light of his renewed interest in me? Or will she concoct another reason to send him away and maintain the masquerade she's constructed? I have no answers, but one thing is certain. I absolutely must shut down his advances immediately. It's crucial that he have no lingering hope about anything forming between us.

If he simply knew the truth, everything would be so much easier, but Zeno was clear on that point. If I break his trust and share a secret he's guarded for half his life, I'll risk losing him forever. I'm not sure he'd ever forgive me. Twenty-four hours earlier, that might not have bothered me. But now? Everything has changed.

ONCE I'M ALONE INSIDE, I grab a bag of frozen broccoli from the freezer because I don't have the mental or physical energy for a baggie and ice. The running wore me out, but it's the emotional exhaustion that leaves me bone-weary. Each step up to my bedroom requires a pep talk and burst of energy that I can only summon with a sheer force of will. A desperation to hide myself away.

After closing the bedroom door behind me, I crawl onto the bed and prop myself against the pillows Gia has artfully arranged against the headboard. She makes the bed each morning like clockwork. Mom never required us to make our beds, so I'm not sure why Gia does it. Routine? A sense of order? Whatever the reason, the bed is made, and I don't feel like undoing it. I toss the bag of broccoli over my ankle and allow my body to sink into the blue and white quilted bedding.

I wish my thoughts were so easily subdued.

My eyes lose focus as I stare out the window and think of my father. The man I've idolized my entire life has been the measuring stick I compare all others to. I've only recently learned how loveless my parents' marriage has been, and now I have to adjust my image of him again to include the taint of infidelity.

I'm old enough to understand that no one is perfect, but this is my daddy. The pedestal I've crafted for him is exceptionally tall. Leaving Mom would have been one thing, but cheating on her is another. I wouldn't wish that on anyone. Nevio and I are not even six months apart in age. No matter how things went down, that fact doesn't paint my father in a flattering light. Mom may make me crazy, but even she doesn't deserve that kind of betrayal.

And what does the affair say about sweet Elena? She had to have known my mother was pregnant with me when she was intimate with my father. Did that bother her? What did her infidelity say about her own marriage? I don't know how to reconcile what I've learned with what I thought to be true.

No matter how much we think we know people, the truth is, we see what they want us to see.

There will always be parts of ourselves we keep hidden

from everyone. The darkest parts that we hope will never see the light of day. But all it takes is the smallest deviation from routine to pull open the curtains and shine a glaring spotlight on our transgressions. That's what happened the day Zeno went to look for his old Game Boy after I'd whined about the game he and his brother were playing. He discovered our parents' secret affair but chose to keep it in the dark until today. Until he offered me a look behind the curtain at a sight I cannot ever unsee.

The knowledge is hard enough for me to process as an adult. I knew my parents were no longer in love, but an affair? That's so much harder to comprehend. I can't imagine how hard it must have been on Zeno to carry that burden as a child. In a way, I understand why he hated my family. My heart aches for him, but at the same time, his justification doesn't erase the hurt he caused for so many years with each slighted insult and cold shoulder.

My emotions have split into two opposing camps. Empathy and remorse war with anger and blame, and I can't tell which is the dominant force. Do I want to scream at Zeno for hurting me or beg his forgiveness for assuming the worst of him?

He'd so consistently dismissed me in all our exchanges that I'd given in and labeled him arrogant and heartless. I'd written off my suspicions that something major had happened to change him, even though I'd been there the day the change came about. I knew something was wrong that had nothing to do with me, but he'd worn me down with his arctic confrontations, and I eventually abandoned my faith in him.

*You're not loyal; you're arrogant and pathetic.*

My own hate-filled words come back to haunt me. I had a valid reason for my venomous attack, not unlike his own reasons for his treatment of me, but that doesn't make me feel any better about what I said.

We've both been wrong.

Both said awful, spiteful things to one another over the years.

So where does that leave us?

And what about Nevio? As far as I can tell, he's been the greatest victim of the whole charade. Mom and Silvano were cheated on, but if the De Rossi marriage was anything like my parents', Silvano had to have known his marriage was less than perfect. It's not an excuse for cheating, but they were adults willingly staying in compromised relationships.

Nevio had been an innocent child.

He'd had no control over his parentage, nor was he given the decency of an explanation to help him understand the situation. To know why he was sent away and why his brother grew so distant. Instead, Nevio was made to feel like an outsider in his own home. I can't imagine how painful that was. No secret is worth that kind of damage.

I slip my hand into the back pocket of my jeans and pull out Zeno's folded letter. The previously crisp pages are now supple with a hint of moisture from my run. My eyes trace over his flowing script. I can envision him at his father's desk, bent with intensity as he pours out his deepest, darkest secrets for me.

*It pained me to even put the words on paper, but you needed to hear the truth.*

*I needed you to know the truth.*

*I have spent a lifetime keeping secrets and covering for people, but I'm glad to share this with you, even if only for your own protection.*

As I read over the last paragraphs for a second time, I get a sense of finality as realization dawns. The primary reason his letter broke me into pieces wasn't the secret he conveyed. The greatest source of my turmoil is in the underlying message. It is the same reason he wrote instead of telling me in person and the reason he left Hardwick for the city.

Zeno De Rossi's letter is his way of saying goodbye.

I told him that he was the last man I'd ever want to be with, and he respected my wishes by walking away. It's an honorable response to my anger, yet my heart feels like it's been wrapped in barbed wire, tangled and bleeding with no way to break free.

After so many years of hurt, I should be glad that he's told me the truth, but somehow, I only feel worse. For the suffering all around me. For the lost years and needless tears. For the man who has always been just out of my reach.

They say the truth sets you free, but it can't undo the past.

So, I ask again, where does that leave us?

I spend hours staring out my bedroom window without arriving at an answer. Sounds filter upstairs as my family returns home. Gia checks on me briefly, disposing of the soggy bag of broccoli. She doesn't push me to talk, though she can tell something has happened. The smell of garlic and pasta wafts upstairs, but not even the tempting aromas can lure me from my solitude. Eventually, golden streaks of sunset cast the trees in stark relief. The light shifts and fades as the sun descends, immersing me in a darkness I welcome with open arms.

# CHAPTER 2

WHEN I WAKE THE NEXT MORNING, MY HAND IMMEDIATELY reaches for my phone. I'm not sure why. I have no reason to expect a message from Zeno, but I look for one anyway. My breathing hitches when a notification shows a missed message, but it's only Grace telling me she's chosen an apartment in the city. I can't summon even feigned interest, so I drop the phone back on my nightstand without responding.

Gia stirs behind me. Her hand lifts to run comforting fingers through my hair. "You want to talk about it?" she asks softly.

*If only I could.*

Even if Zeno hadn't asked for my silence, my emotions are still so jagged and raw that spilling them aloud would be more than I could bear. However, should I decide to divulge what I learned at a later point in time, Gia would be the first person I'd turn to. I trust her absolutely.

But for now, I shake my head and feel grateful that Gia is so patient. Had I found her nearly catatonic in our bed last night as she'd found me, I would have demanded an explanation. My worry would have trampled her need for space, but my sister is hypersensitive to those around her. She is able to shelf her concerns and give a wealth of grace with a simple hug.

She offers the perfect support with one arm draped over me and her body curved around mine. Once I've absorbed all the love I can handle without summoning more tears, I sit up and give her a weary smile. "Thank you, G."

"I'm here for you whenever you're ready."

I give her arm a squeeze and stand, noting that my ankle has improved greatly in the night. It's stiff but not terribly sore. I grab a change of clothes, walking gingerly so as not to risk further injury, and head for the bathroom. The entire time, I keep my right fist tightly clasped around the letter I held throughout the night. I don't release the crumpled paper until I'm safely locked in the bathroom. It's time to respect Zeno's wishes and dispose of his message before it's accidentally discovered.

I open it one last time, only pausing from my task briefly to note my filthy reflection. I didn't even put on pajamas last night, let alone shower. I didn't care then, and I don't care now. My attention is solely focused on the pages suspended between my trembling fingers.

I turn on the shower to start the water warming and to

drown out the sounds I'm about to make. Turning to the last page, I tear away the bottom portion containing his final words.

*I wish you the best.*
*Z*

I set the small scrap of paper aside before shredding the rest of the letter and depositing the strips into the toilet. One flush later, the letter is gone—all but his parting words. Those, I tuck into the pocket of the clean leggings I plan to wear. I'm not sure why I've kept the shred of paper. I'm still upset with Zeno in a number of ways, but I'm also a little scared he'll never be a part of my life again. Even when he was an ass, he was still there, asking my dad about me or giving condescending advice. All I know is that if this is where our paths permanently diverge, then I want to take a piece of him with me.

I shower longer than normal, scrubbing away thoughts and emotions until I'm adequately numb for my day. Working at Hardwick will be a challenge when everything around me serves as a reminder of thoughts I wish to ignore. To stay strong and unaffected, I'll need to ensure my defenses remain intact. I promise myself I'll avoid people whenever possible, keep busy at all times, and stay far, far away from all things Zeno.

I'm remarkably successful throughout the morning, maintaining a machine-like trance until lunch. I'm so diligent in my earnest attempt to keep my mind preoccupied that I don't notice Nevio watching me until his playful voice snags my attention.

"It's twelve thirty, Isa. Even if you don't want lunch, that ankle could probably use a rest." He smirks at me lightheartedly from where he leans against the dining room doorframe.

I pull out my phone and confirm that he's right. "I didn't realize it'd gotten so late." I toss my polishing rag onto the tray I'd been working on and survey my progress. Cecelia mentioned polishing the silver when I started working at Hardwick, and I figured today was an ideal day to begin the mammoth undertaking.

Nevio closes the distance between us and reaches for my hand. "Let's grab a sandwich."

I pull back and raise my hands for him to see. "Careful, I'm covered in silver polish." In truth, I don't want him touching me in any way, but the sticky polish is an easy excuse.

"I'll survive," he says wryly, clasping my hand and tugging me away from the table. "That ankle feeling better, I take it?"

*So much for avoiding touching him.* I've got to say something. This can't continue.

He's still courting the idea of a relationship between us. I don't want to lead him on, but I'm not sure how to pull away without hurting him. He's been nothing but sweet to me since he returned home.

"Yeah. I made sure to ice and rest it," I answer.

*Come on, Isa. Put your big girl panties on and set him straight.*

"Good, but just to be safe, I want you to have a seat, and I'll get us lunch." Nevio pulls out a chair at the kitchen table and motions for me to sit. "I believe there's pastrami and turkey—one of those sound better than the other?"

"Pastrami sounds good." I'm not hungry, but I'll eat anyway. I don't want him asking questions.

"Same, that makes it easy." He winks.

My stomach cinches even tighter. My only consolation is that his lighthearted mood might make this a tiny bit easier. I open my mouth to shatter his hopes of a relationship between us, but the words don't come forth.

"Am I allowed to get us drinks?" I say instead. "Or would that get me in trouble?" My tone is playful purely from awkwardness, but I know he'll misinterpret and think I'm flirting. *God, what a mess.*

"You stay put. I've got it covered."

"If you say so."

"I do say so. I need you to be better by Thursday."

My heart rate kicks into a jog. "Oh, yeah? Why's that?"

"Because a friend of mine is having a party, and I want you to go with me. It's hard to dance with a bad ankle. We have never danced together, and there's nothing I'd like more." He cuts a glance at me briefly between layering the pastrami on Kaiser rolls.

*Shit.* This is exactly what I wanted to avoid. I've been gently giving him the slip even before I found out the truth, but he's still in pursuit. My desire to avoid conflict is urging me to keep making excuses until he gives up. I'm tongue-tied and obliging despite the crucial importance of putting distance between us. But it's disrespectful to leave him guessing and toy with his emotions. Haven't I spent the past twenty-four hours judging others for not being honest with him? How am I any better if I take the coward's way out instead of being up front and telling him truthfully that a relationship between us isn't meant to be?

I sit in silence as I debate my next move. My lack of response is enough to put him on guard. He brings over a plate for each of us and joins me at the table but makes no move to eat.

"You have something against parties?"

"No, it's just that ... I want to make sure we're on the same page."

"And what page is that?"

*Here goes nothing.*

I meet his deep mahogany gaze. His eyes narrow at the apology he must see in my eyes. "I enjoy hanging out with you—I always have—but I don't want you to get the wrong impression."

"Wrong impression? What impression am I supposed to get when you leaned into our kiss? You went to dinner with me, and your face lights up whenever I see you. Exactly what impression did you mean to send?"

*Goddammit.* He's not wrong, but things have changed.

"My head has been a mess with my mom's stuff, and I know I've sent some mixed signals, which is why I wanted to clear things up. I don't want to hurt you, and I'm so glad we've gotten back in touch. I don't want to lose that."

Nevio slowly crosses his arms over his chest, ramping up the tension surrounding us. "This has to do with Zeno, doesn't it?" His hushed question drips with disgust.

"No," I urge quickly. "This has nothing to do with

him." I lean forward and place my hand flat against the table halfway between us. A plea. A bid for understanding.

My words bounce right off him like rain on a tin roof. "Mom told me she thought something was going on between you two. I didn't believe her because I've seen the way he's treated you. I knew you had too much self-respect to demean yourself like that." His lips lift in a snarl, and I pull back, growing defensive as his response morphs into a personal attack.

"I'm telling you my decision has nothing to do with him. If you don't believe me, that's *your* problem."

Cruelty twists his lips into a vicious scowl. "My only problem was finding a way to loosen that vise around your puritanical knees. We've known each other our whole lives, and it's taken weeks to get a fucking kiss. As far as I'm concerned, I should thank you for saving me the headache of going any further. Besides, I have no interest in my brother's leftovers."

My mouth hangs open as Nevio strolls from the room as though he didn't just spit in my face. Never in a million years would I have expected his reaction. A bruised ego is one thing. His calculated attack came deep from a cesspool of bitterness I'd never dreamed lay inside him. Was the animosity a product of the lies he'd been subjected to? Nevio claimed Z had treated him poorly, but I'd never been witness to any behavior by him or their parents to justify such residual hatred. Where had such spite come from? The mere hint that I'd chosen his brother over him had eliminated all rational thought.

I shake my head, finally hinging my jaw shut as my shock wears off.

I'm disappointed that he could say such awful things, but mostly I'm just sad for him. Nevio is more damaged than I realized. I hate that for him, but it also helps ease the sting of his attack. His reaction is a reflection of his own issues, making me wonder what made him so bitter.

My father had warned me about him. It would make sense that Dad was trying to keep me from dating my own brother, but maybe there was more to his warning. Zeno and my dad both hinted that Nevio was trouble. I'd told myself both men had been overreacting for one reason or another. I'd known Nevio so well when we were children, and it seemed like he hadn't changed a bit. His charm does a remarkable job of hiding the scars that mar his personality, but they're still there beneath the surface, mottled and raw.

I think back to Zeno's letter. He indicated that Nevio had lied about Zeno asking him not to come to their father's funeral. Such a falsehood isn't so hard to imagine anymore. I have to wonder how else Nevio might have massaged the truth to paint himself in a better light.

It's no wonder the two brothers are no longer close.

And to think of how accusatory I'd been about the way Zeno treated his brother. Neither man is faultless, but I had no business inserting my own misguided opinions. My self-righteous judgments. In that regard, at the very least, I owe Z an apology.

Slipping my phone from my back pocket, I check for missed messages.

Nothing.

My emotions are only slightly more settled than they were when I woke up this morning, but it's enough to give me direction. I need to know whether Zeno is still willing to talk to me.

When I open our text thread, I expect to type a short apology, but that's not what comes out. I try not to overthink the three simple words because while they're not an apology, they need to be said. I'm starting a conversation with him. That's the important part—that and speaking from my heart. Everything else is out of my hands, so there's no point in worrying over it.

**Me: You hurt me.**

I hit send and only have to wait a minute for his reply.

**Zeno: That is my one greatest regret in life.**

And with those few simple words, a bandage wraps gently over the wounds scattered across my heart. They've been unable to fully heal since he first kicked me out of Hardwick so many years ago. His remorse without caveat or explanation means more to me than he could ever know.

In addition, the tiny thread of communication between us reassures me that all is not lost. I may not know what else to say or where we go from here, but I know there is hope.

Hope for clarity and honesty.

Hope for trust and maybe even reconciliation.

To what end, I don't know, but the prospect is enticing. And if the mere possibility of a connection with Zeno brings me joy, then I should do what I can to explore that outcome. Considering our rocky past, any kind of relationship between us would be a challenge—friendship or otherwise. We are both lugging around enough baggage to ground a jetliner. But is a challenge necessarily bad? What if he and I could reach a place beyond our past? Wouldn't that be worth the obstacles we might encounter? When I think of the Zeno I used to look up to—the boy who befriended and protected me—the answer is a resounding yes.

# CHAPTER 3

I don't see Nevio again before leaving work. My afternoon is spent elbow-deep in silver polish, but the thoughts that accompany me are noticeably improved. When Gia informs me that we received a dinner invitation from the Larsons the day prior, I initially consider declining simply to avoid the burden of conversation. But by quitting time, I'm relieved to find that the prospect of socializing isn't as overwhelming as it had felt earlier in the day. I'm much improved, despite my tiff with Nevio. When I first lumbered from bed with the weight of the world on my shoulders, I would have thought it would take far more than a single text to shift my mood. But Zeno has always had that effect on me. No matter how securely I anchor myself, I will always feel the pull of his current.

After stopping home for a few minutes to freshen up,

we all make our way to the Larson cottage. All of us except for Livia, who is yet again missing in action. Fine by me. My tolerance for drama is at an all-time low. And dinner with the Larsons isn't a grand occasion. Our families have hosted one another at least once a month for as long as I can remember. My parents sometimes host, but dinner is often at the Larson's house. Considering neither of my parents is particularly fond of cooking, and the house is usually a mess, our reciprocity is somewhat lopsided. Fortunately, Mrs. Larson adores having company.

Their family welcomes us with warm greetings and the delicious aroma of a slow-cooked pot roast. Grace is all smiles. She's even wearing a touch of makeup, which is unusual for her.

"You look gorgeous, Gracy! You'll have to tell me all about the apartment you picked." My joy for her is genuine, and I do everything I can to suppress my fears that her house of cards will come crashing down. I don't ask her about Aldo, the disgusting bookie/loan shark who helped finance her move to the city. I don't want to think about him at all, so I don't.

"Absolutely, but I have even more good news to share! I got a job!" she squeals quietly, hands clapping together with excitement.

"Oh, my God, that's *wonderful*! Where will you be working?"

"It was kind of a long shot, so I can't believe I got it, but I'll be ushering at Broadway plays! I put in applications for all kinds of positions, and I may still need to do some waitressing as well, but this kind of job was what I was really hoping for. I'll get discounted tickets for most shows and can watch the shows when I'm working for free. The head ushers who run everything actually make decent money. I'd love to work toward that someday."

"That sounds incredible, Grace. I'm so happy for you!" I give her a hug with a wide grin. Her optimism is infectious, and it nurtures my ravaged psyche. "When do you start?"

"They want me as soon as I'm able, and the apartment is already available, so I'll be moving this weekend. It's all come together so fast that my head is spinning. That's why we're having dinner during the week instead of Friday or Saturday. Dad is going to help me move this weekend. It shouldn't be too bad, though. I don't have all that much stuff to move." She proceeds to tell me all about her studio apartment and her plans to make her transition as smooth as possible. "I suppose it's good I'm leaving since we don't know if the Bishops will be coming back. Mom and Dad may be looking for new work as well."

I hadn't even thought about them. I'd been so focused on Gia's heartbreak that I hadn't considered how the Bishops' departure would affect the Larsons.

"That would be awful—they've been working at the estate forever. Has Carter not given them any hint at his intentions?" It's a question I should have asked ages ago. If anyone knew what Bishop was doing, it would be his estate manager.

She shakes her head. "No. He told them he wasn't sure when or if he'd be back, but there's been no word since. Dad keeps assuring Mom that it'll be fine, but I can tell he's worried, too."

I wonder if Zeno realizes his interference in Gia and Carter's budding relationship has affected so many lives. And for what? His fear that the couple would end up like his parents? He may have been right regarding his warning about Nevio, but he overstepped his bounds where Carter Bishop was concerned. He should never have meddled in their relationship, and I have an urge to tell him so, but it will have to wait.

Dinner passes quickly in the company of longtime friends. Grace's parents share their excitement for their firstborn, leading to stories from everyone about first venturing from home. The food is delicious, as always. Ordinarily, we would stay until at least ten, but with work the next morning, we head home at a reasonable hour. Everyone else heads inside to start getting ready for bed, but I linger on the back porch and take out my phone. Enjoying my evening didn't diminish my need to tell him how upset I am over his role in Carter leaving. He explained his perspective about warning Carter away from Gia in his letter, but I need him to know that I still disagree with what he did.

**Me: We had dinner at the Larson's tonight.**

It's a bit random, but I'm not sure how else to introduce the subject.

**Zeno: How was it?**

**Me: Good except they're worried about their jobs.**

**Me: It wasn't your place to come between Carter and my sister. They aren't your parents.**

The conversation dots appear then quickly disappear

before my phone buzzes with an incoming call. Zeno's name flashes on the screen, and I swipe to answer.

"Hey," I say softly. "You didn't have to call."

"I did. This subject is too complicated for text. I take it your sister is still upset?" His voice is warm molasses heating me from the inside out. It's my turn to talk, but I wish I could sit back and listen all night to the honey-tipped tenor of his words instead.

"She is, but there's so much more to consider. They're really worried about whether Carter will come back and if they'll lose their jobs if he sells the place."

A deep swell of breath comes across the line. "Sometimes, there are unfortunate consequences to our actions. I was concerned for a friend and voiced that concern. I don't regret that decision. There are many things to apologize for, but I still don't believe that's one of them. If his affection for her was delicate enough to be doused by our brief conversation, then that is an issue all its own."

"That's not entirely true. Carter and Gia aren't like you or me. We're headstrong and stubborn, and for the most part, confident in our actions. They're different. Shyness and reserve make it harder for them to form attachments, especially with someone as equally timid. People like them struggle to make lasting relationships. While they're steadfast and loyal once a connection is forged, those early days are exceedingly fragile."

"Yet you're convinced that they suit one another?"

"I am. They would be considerate and uniquely devoted to each other if given that chance."

"I didn't think you knew Carter so well to make that kind of call."

"I know enough, and I trust my sister's judgment. She's never been so attached to anyone."

"I'll have to take your word for it. She never seems overly interested in him from my perspective," he admits warily.

"She's reserved with her emotions. Even I sometimes struggle to interpret how she's feeling, and I've known her since birth."

Zeno huffs. "I suppose I should admire her reserve, but it sure makes reading her difficult."

"You're one to talk," I tease softly, then take a deep breath as the direction of our conversation shifts. I hadn't expected to text him about my exchange with Nevio, but now that he's on the phone, I feel the words need to be said. "I spoke with Nevio today."

Z is quiet for several long seconds. "And what did you discuss?"

"He wanted me to go to a party with him. I'd already decided before your letter that I wasn't interested, but with my new perspective, I knew that I needed to be up front with him. He's been very ... attentive, and I didn't want to lead him on."

"I'd like to think he'd respect your decision, but I doubt it."

"It was awful, Z." My voice grows thin and small as I recall the hurtful words Nevio spat at me.

The line is dead silent before Zeno's ragged growl touches my ear. "Did he fucking touch you?"

I shake my head, though he can't see me. "No, but the things he said—they were terrible. It was like he became a complete stranger all of a sudden, spewing such hateful things. I knew he used his charm on people, but I had no idea ... I had no clue that the person underneath had become so ugly."

"He's not who you think he is, Luisa."

"I can see that now." I stand and begin to pace on the back porch as awkwardness sets in. "Anyway, I just wanted you to know, and ... I want to say that ... I'm sorry. I should have apologized already, but it's been a lot to take in. I said some really awful things to you when I didn't know the whole picture. I assumed the worst of you, and though the truth hasn't erased all my anger and hurt, it helps to understand."

"You couldn't have known why I behaved the way I did," he says fervently. "The whole thing has been a shit situation for too long. You have every right to be upset."

I don't know what to say. Zeno is being considerate and civil, and even though I want to gobble up his attention, a part of me is still waiting for the other shoe to drop. For him to snap out of his temporary insanity and remember that he wants nothing to do with me.

Will I ever be able to trust him again like I did when we were young? Only time will tell. That type of faith and connection would have to be reforged, and a new bond created.

"I know you don't want the affair to get out," I say, broaching a sensitive subject. "But do you think it would help Nevio to know? To understand?"

"Knowing about that would only make things worse."

I can't imagine how that could be right, but he knows Nevio's issues and past better than I do. My pious assumptions have already gotten me into trouble once, so I'm not about to make that same mistake again so soon. "That's too bad, but I guess at this point, there are no easy fixes."

"Unfortunately, no."

The phone line hums with an awkward silence as our discussion wanes, though neither of us seems eager to end the call.

"Well, I better get going," I finally concede. "It's getting late."

"Of course, you should get some rest."

"Good night, Z," I whisper.

"Isa…" He pauses, and I wait with bated breath to hear his next words. "I'm glad we talked."

"Me, too."

"Sleep well. I'll be in touch."

I end the call with a blossoming smile sprouting straight from my heart. I feel like we've taken the first step down a new path. A thrilling and promising new path that is so unexpected, it's also a little terrifying. Do I dare get my hopes up? Could I quash them even if I wanted to? I doubt it, judging by the electric energy now thrumming in my veins. My train is already headed down the tracks. All I can do now is proceed with caution.

Inside, my dad is watching TV alone in the living room. I tell him good night and head upstairs to find Gia cuddled under the covers, playing a mindless game on her phone.

"Hey there." My smile grows as I join her on the bed.

Her face lights up, clearly relieved at my improved mood. "Hey! You feeling better?"

"I'm getting there. It's been a crazy couple of days. Hell, it's been a crazy few weeks." I lie down next to her, and she follows suit, turning on her side to face me.

"You want to tell me about it?"

I do, but I deliberate for a moment before going forward. I know by telling Gia this secret, I'm technically breaking Zeno's trust. However, I can guarantee with absolute certainty that she will go to her grave before she tells anyone. I need to be able to talk to someone about what I've learned, and there is no better secret-keeper than Gia. And after all, this secret involves her, too.

"What I'm about to tell you cannot be breathed to another living soul. I was told under the strictest of confidences."

Surprise widens her eyes. "Maybe you shouldn't say anything, then. I don't want you to break anyone's trust."

"It's not that simple. This involves all of us, and I need to talk about it with *someone*."

"Okay." She nods for me to go on.

"After we got back from the city, Zeno came by the house."

"He did?"

"I was on the back porch, so he didn't come inside. We talked, and it didn't go well. Actually, it was more like a fight. The next day, he left a letter for me finally explaining what happened when we were kids and why he's been so distant ever since."

"What happened?" She lifts onto her elbow expectantly. "What could possibly justify the way he's behaved?"

"You're not going to believe this." I lean in and speak on a hushed breath. "Dad had an affair with Elena, and Nevio is their son. He's not technically a De Rossi. He's our half brother."

Gia drifts slowly back down to her pillow, wide eyes turning to the ceiling. "Holy shit."

I have to bite down on my lips to keep from laughing. Gia rarely cusses. And though this is a serious matter, hearing her swear always tickles me.

I've pulled the rug out from under her. I know the feeling well. Only, she wasn't embroiled with the brothers like I was. For her, the news may be a little distressing, but it's more fascinating than anything.

"That's why Zeno tried to keep Nevio away from me," I continue. "It's also why he's been so rude. He said that for the longest time that I reminded him of Dad, who he blamed for tearing apart his family."

"Oh, Isa. That's terrible. I mean, I can see why he'd feel that way, but the whole thing is just awful."

"He's known all this time but never told anyone. Fourteen years."

Her brows draw together over compassionate brown eyes. "That had to be so hard on Z to carry that burden as a child."

"Yeah, but not telling anyone meant Nevio was sent away in high school solely because he had a crush on me, though he wasn't told as much. He felt like he was being cast out. That hurt him so much, and now ... Gia, he's terribly bitter.

I didn't realize, but today when I told him I wasn't interested in a relationship, he showed his true colors. It would have broken your heart. He's so angry with the world."

"I imagine Z did the best he could at the time. We can't expect a young teenager to know how to navigate something like that." Always compassionate, that's my sister.

"I know. I hate for someone who was so good-natured to become twisted with spite, especially if simple honesty could have prevented it."

"You don't know if that would have helped. Some people become bitter for no reason at all, and others have all the reason in the world but choose to remain unjaded by life's misfortunes."

God, I love my sister. I may begrudge her perspective at times, but for the most part, she is insightful beyond belief. I hadn't considered that Zeno's secret isn't necessarily the sole cause of Nevio's issues. The two seem so naturally connected, but I have no proof that's the case.

I pull her into a hug. "You're the best, G. I'm sorry I wasn't up for talking yesterday. I needed a chance to process things."

"You know I'm always here for you. And don't worry about the secret. I won't tell a soul."

When I ease away, Gia shakes her head dazedly.

"Dad and Elena. Who would have thought?"

"Crazy, right? Guess I can cross Ancestry.com off the Christmas gift list." I cut my eyes over to her, and we both burst into laughter—a cathartic, healing, hysterical laughter totally inappropriate for the moment but exactly what we need.

I drift into a peaceful sleep that night, my heart lighter than it's felt in weeks. Things are looking up, and I can only hope that my luck has turned a corner. Before I know it, I'll be finishing school, and this chaotic summer will be a distant memory.

# CHAPTER 4

Gia and I talk again on Wednesday once she's had a chance to digest what she learned. Other than our discussions, the day is blessedly free of drama. Thursday follows in a similar fashion, except when evening rolls around, I'm surprised by a text from Zeno.

**Zeno: I was hoping we could talk in person this weekend, but Christiano asked me to join him in the Hamptons for a meeting.**

I smile at his text. He didn't have to tell me his plans, especially where Christiano was concerned. He's the boss of the Giordano crime family—Zeno's boss—and I know better than to expect Z to tell me anything about that aspect of his life.

As I begin to type, a trickle of doubt creeps into my mind. Does Z actually have a reason to stay away, or is he avoiding me? If that was the case, why reach out at all? Maybe he's reconsidering his feelings and trying to slowly back away.

I try to calm the doubts and take him at his word, but years of discord between us makes that difficult.

**Me: We can always talk next week. It's been good to have time to think.**

**Zeno: Just so you know, I've ordered Nevio to the city. He shouldn't be back at Hardwick anytime soon.**

I'm not sure how to respond, verbally or emotionally. I hate for Nevio to be kept from his home, but I can't deny the relief of knowing I won't run into him at the house. That possibility hung in the back of my mind over the past two days and kept me slightly on edge. Nevio wouldn't hurt me—not physically, anyway—but I don't want to argue with him either. Not if he's going to turn ugly. I assume the reason he hasn't reached out to apologize is that he's still upset. I'd hoped he'd come to his senses by now, but that doesn't appear to be the case.

**Me: I haven't heard from him. Not sure if that's good or bad.**

**Zeno: It's good, trust me.**

**Me: Will you tell me what happened to him?**

I may be butting in, but if Z wants open communication between us, then I need to be free to ask questions.

**Zeno: Some things are better left in the dark, but if you really want to know, I'll tell you next time I see you.**

**Me: I would appreciate that.** *For the information and for not being upset that I asked.*

**Zeno: Anything, Isa. All you ever need to do is ask.**

What I wouldn't give to feel the rumble of those words spoken against my skin. To see the veracity on his face and truly believe his declaration. As it is, I stare at the digital screen like a child pining for the toys in a store window, unsure how to make it happen. To truly believe all of it could be mine.

Fortunately, Z saves me the uncertain task of coming up with a response.

**Zeno: I'm having dinner with some colleagues, so I have to go, but text if you need me.**

*Text if you need me.* It's like he's reading my mind, saying all the things I've always wanted to hear from him. It feels too good to be true, except it is true, if I can find the courage to believe him. To step off that ledge and trust that he'll catch me.

**Me: I will. Enjoy dinner.**

**Zeno: Good night, Isa.**

And I do have a good night, that is until a noise wakes me around three o'clock. Gia is still sleeping soundly beside me, but my brain is whirring like the blades of a fan as I lay in the dark, waiting for the noise again. When a thud resounds from the bathroom, I realize that Livia has most likely woken me, yet again, after one of her not-so-stealthy returns from a night out. The last time she woke me, she was drunk and hardly able to undress.

I groan quietly and roll from bed. No matter how annoying she may be, she's still my little sister, and I feel the need to check on her. She hasn't locked the door, which is helpful, and I'm pleased to discover that she isn't completely trashed.

"Hey, Isa. Did I wake you?" Her hair is a mess and makeup smudged, but her smile is genuine as she sits on the edge of the tub. She's had a good night.

"Yeah, you're not the quietest drunk," I tease her.

"I'm not even drunk—not anymore, at least. Nevio made sure I drank my water this time." She slips one of her wedge sandals off, eyeing me coyly for my response. She thinks she's teased me with a juicy nugget of gossip, not realizing what she's actually done is drop an atomic-sized bomb on the vinyl bathroom floor.

My heart thunders in my ears as I momentarily forget to breathe. "Livy, you have to listen to me. You *cannot* date Nevio." I move close and drop to my knees so that I'm at eye level with her. The pain in my kneecaps is nothing compared to the overwhelming panic surging in my veins. I have to find a way to make her listen, but I know my sister, and my warning will only make her want him more.

As expected, her initial surprise quickly fades to irritation. "Why the hell not?"

Livia would be the absolute worst person to tell about Nevio's paternity. Everyone in New York would know within the hour. And besides, I already told one more person than I was supposed to. There's no way I can tell her the truth. How can I possibly convince her without telling her that she's dating her own brother?

*Shit. Shit. SHIT!*

"I know he's charming and seems like the perfect catch, but Liv, you have to believe me. Nevio has issues. He's not who you think he is, and I don't want you to get hurt."

"No, you don't want me to land the hottie next door

that you couldn't get for yourself. You're just jealous." She stands and tries to maneuver around me, but I'm on my feet in an instant.

"I'm not jealous, Liv. If I'd wanted a relationship with Nevio, I could have pursued that years ago. I'm trying to protect you as a sister. I'd love for you to be deliriously happy and marry a wealthy man, but Nevio will not give you that. *Please*, listen to me." I clasp her arms and plead with her green eyes, ringed in gold just like our mother's.

She shakes off my hold but avoids my gaze. I've managed to inject a sliver of doubt into her plans.

"I'm not sure any of it matters anyway. He's staying in the city now, so I'm not sure when I'll see him again." She wipes at her eyes with a makeup removing cloth as though she doesn't care one way or another.

I see right through her. Liv would never be so nonchalant about a relationship with a wealthy man.

"He's not trustworthy, and I don't want to be hurt. Did you know he asked me to the party you were at tonight? Hell, he probably asked you in some twisted attempt to get back at me. When I told him the other day that I wasn't interested in going out again, he said some awful things to me. Even if he is truly interested in you, surely you don't want to be with someone who's that two-faced."

"You want me to end up stuck in this house forever, don't you? Whatever happened between you two is irrelevant and only tainting the way you see him. I should have known you wouldn't be happy for me." She tosses the dirty wipe in the trash and turns cold, unfeeling eyes on me. "It's late. I'm going to bed now."

My bumbling attempt at reasoning with her is abruptly shut down when she walks away. I don't sleep the rest of the night. My mind is too busy concocting horrific ways for Livia's new crush to end in disaster. I brainstorm every possible solution I can devise and measure the probability of success. By the time the sun finally peeks through the blinds in our room, I've come to the conclusion that I need help. And not just anyone's help. I need my dad.

I may not be able to tell anyone the secret, but that doesn't stop me from talking to someone who already knows. And it's a safe assumption that Dad knows he's Nevio's biological father. He'll recognize how urgent it is to keep the two of them apart and help without me having to bring up Nevio's paternity. I'll get my help and still mostly keep my promise to Zeno.

I go downstairs early, hoping to catch him before Mom or Gia show up for breakfast. Coffee is my first priority after lying awake for hours. I turn on the Keurig and wish I had access to an espresso. I'm going to need all the caffeine I can get today.

A few sips into my first cup, Dad strolls in from his bedroom with a grin.

"How come you're up so early?"

"Actually, I wanted to talk to you. Can you come outside with me for a minute?"

His face sobers. "Lead the way." He opens the door for me, and I step out into the grass a few feet from the porch. Far enough that we shouldn't be overheard.

"You know how you warned me about Nevio?"

"Yeah?" he asks warily.

"Well, I shut that down, but last night, I learned that Livia went out with him." I watch closely for his reaction. If I tell him outright that I know about his affair, I will have had to explain how I acquired that information. Word would likely travel to Elena that Zeno knows, and he might not want that. I need to play this carefully.

"She's seeing him?"

"They went to a party last night, and she hinted that it wasn't the first time they've gone out." *Read between the lines, Dad. Please, see what I'm getting at without me having to spell it out.*

He kicks at a stick and gives me a smirk. "You know how Livy is. She thinks every man with money is her golden goose. Neither of the De Rossi boys is interested in her. They've known Liv her whole life and never paid her one bit of attention."

"Daddy, things can change. Aren't you worried about her?"

"Not really. You know how she is. She probably begged to go with him hoping to meet friends of his, and he let her tag along."

I gape at him incredulously. How can he be so dismissive about the possible dangers? He has to know, doesn't he? How could he not? Even if Elena didn't tell him Nevio was his, surely, he could see his own eyes looking back at him—the same way Zeno figured it out. Once a person knows of the affair, the resemblance between father and son is hard to miss.

But then again, if he *did* know, how could he blow off a

potentially incestuous relationship between his children? There's no way he'd be so casual about it. A stream of curses vulgar enough to make a sailor blush fires through my mind. Dad won't be assisting me as I'd hoped. His hands-off approach to parenting was always a little annoying where my younger sisters were concerned, but this is plain maddening. With Livia still living at home, Dad's leverage over her would be enormously helpful. All I can do now is hope that Nevio returning to the city will limit their interaction, but it's not a guarantee.

I meet my dad's sad eyes pleadingly. "I get that you're not worried, but I am, and it would mean a lot to me if you'd help me discourage her from hanging around him."

Dad cups his hands around my upper arms and gives them a gentle squeeze. "Of course, Lulu, if you're that worried about it. Your mom mentioned wanting to hit Macy's on Saturday, and I had somewhere I wanted to stop in as well. What if she and I take the girls and spend a weekend in the city? We'll keep them busy, and you and Gia can have a little time alone. It's not a permanent solution, but it's a start."

I fling myself into his arms, relieved to have any help I can get. "Thank you, Daddy."

"Don't mention it. It's been ages since I've been out of here. It'll do me some good."

The back door opens, and I pull away to see Mom watching us curiously.

"What's all this about?"

"Just hugging my daughter," Dad answers. "I'm allowed to do that, aren't I?"

"Sure, you are, but you two look suspicious doing it out here in the yard when the sun's hardly up."

"I was telling Luisa that I thought I'd take you and the younger girls into the city this weekend. We can leave after work this evening."

Mom's face lights up, all her nosy curiosity forgotten. "I'll get Chiara on the phone and let her know we're coming!" She dashes inside to call her sister-in-law. Dad and I follow her inside and resume our morning routines, my shoulders already feeling lighter. It's not a permanent fix, but it's a start. Between Gia, Dad, Zeno, and myself, surely we can keep them from disaster.

While Gia and I walk to Hardwick some thirty minutes later, I tell her about Livia and Nevio.

"You think Mom and Dad will be vigilant with her this weekend?" Gia asks. "If he's in the city, there's a chance she'll try to slip away and meet up with him. Dad doesn't have a great track record of keeping tabs on her, and Mom would cheer her on. If Dad doesn't know the real reason you're worried, he won't be overly strict."

"That's crossed my mind as well. I'd like to think Dad won't let her go off on her own, but I'm not certain."

"One of us who knows the truth needs to be near her at all times until her infatuation wears off. I should go with them and make sure nothing happens." Gia's offer is a huge relief. I'd been contemplating whether I should go with them but was selfishly reluctant.

"Are you sure?" I ask only half-heartedly.

"Yeah. We can check in on Grace, and I'm sure Chiara will have plenty for us to do."

"I really appreciate you doing that. When you get back, we can come up with a monitoring system. I don't think we can trust her an inch."

"Agreed," Gia sighs. "At least this business has taken my mind off Carter." She shrugs, and the hopelessness of it hurts my heart.

"Maybe you can use the trip to take another shot at talking to him." I doubt she'll do it, but I have to suggest it.

Gia just smiles placidly and continues walking.

"I'm supposed to talk to Z on Sunday," I continue. "I can enlist his help as well."

She peers at me from the corner of her eye. "You guys talking?"

This time, I shrug. "A couple of times. We're slowly wading through everything."

"If it means anything, I think you're doing the right thing. I know how much you always adored him growing up and how much it hurt when he pushed you away. It's about time things got worked out between you."

"Let's hope it's a good thing and not more heartbreak waiting to happen. Because if he bails on me again, I might need help disposing of a body." I raise a brow at her playfully.

Gia grins mischievously. "He hurts you again, and I'll gladly bring the shovel."

# CHAPTER 5

Friday night, the house is quiet, and I'm blissfully alone. I thought I would read once everyone left, but I do something unexpected once the house is empty. I get out my idea notebook. I've been jotting down book ideas for years, so an extensive collection of story tidbits is scribbled on the pages. I read through each until I come to my notes from nearly a decade before, when I still spent time wondering why Z pushed me away. The change in him had been so abrupt, I'd channeled the trending *Twilight* books to develop a fanciful theory about what had happened. I hypothesized that he'd been transformed into a vampire and was pushing me away to protect me from himself. It had been a childish escape from the truth, but the story idea suddenly intrigues me and takes on new life now that our story has further unfolded.

Before I know it, my stomach is growling, and I've written ten pages outlining a vampire romance that captures my soul. The story materialized before my eyes. The basic plot is the same as I'd first envisioned, but I'm able to add depth and complexity now that my imagination has the benefit of experience.

I adore the alternate reality I've created.

When I finally head to bed, I go to sleep with the satisfaction of believing for the first time that I might actually make my publishing dreams a reality. I have never felt so damn proud of myself.

I wake early with enthusiasm the next morning, excited to dive back into the creative process. I spend hours on the couch developing my characters and the fantasy world in which their story unfolds. Normally, stress inhibits my creativity, but the chaos of my life has somehow inspired me. The release of ideas is invigorating, and the escape from reality is more than welcome.

When my phone rings close to noon, I grumble until I see Grace's face flash on the screen.

"Hey!" I greet her excitedly. "How's the new apartment coming along?"

"It's the size of a shoebox, but it's mine, and I love it!"

"That's awesome!"

"Yeah, but there's more. I didn't want to say anything until I knew how it went, but Ari called last week. We went to dinner last night." A radiant smile colors her words with happiness. I don't have to see it to know it's there.

"Oh my God, Grace! That's wonderful! I take it the evening went well?"

"It was perfect. I told her that the whole scene was new to me, and she was happy to take things slow. We had such a great time together. She's coming by tomorrow to help me finish setting up the apartment. There's not actually that much to do, but she offered, and I like the idea of showing her my new place."

"Honey, I'm so incredibly happy for you. So many exciting new adventures!"

"It's a lot at once, but I'm so happy about everything. I have two months until I'm supposed to have Aldo paid, and I don't think that will be an issue since I got that job already. Everything has come together perfectly."

"I'll offer one bit of advice. It may sound paranoid, but take someone with you when you give him the money. I'm even happy to come to the city if you need me." I can't help but warn her again. She seems to have everything under control, but I worry.

"Okay, I'll make sure to do that. Sorry to keep this short and sweet, but I'm meeting Gia for lunch. I just wanted to keep you posted on the Ari situation as I promised."

"I'm so glad you did! Enjoy your lunch!"

We say our goodbyes, and I end the call with a buoyancy in my chest that I haven't felt in ages. There are still plenty of worries I could dwell upon if I was so inclined but also an equal number of reasons to be optimistic for the future. Grace, my budding career as an author, and even the fragile reconstruction of a relationship I had thought was irreparable.

I choose to be optimistic and focus on the rays of light peeking through the clouds.

By the time the sun has set on my Saturday, I'm two glasses into a bottle of rosé and dancing around the living room to Britney Spears's "Toxic." I have a dance-off with myself, drowning in a release of endorphins like I haven't felt in months. Even once I give into fatigue and slump onto the couch, the pulsing strains of music from my youth keep my spirits floating high. Eyes closed. Hand waving in the air. I am the embodiment of contentment. I am the music that fills my ears, keeping me from hearing when my little party of one doubles in size. It's not until I open my eyes to skip a song that I realize I'm no longer alone.

I see his reflection first.

Outlined against the black television screen, the form of a man leaning against the entry wall behind me catches my eye. I instantly snap from my tipsy state of relaxation and bolt from the sofa. My motion jars the coffee table, knocking over my half-full glass of wine, but I pay it no mind. Every ounce of my attention is glued to the menacing man who has broken into my house and now stares at me with a drunken gleam in his eye. A vulgar, depraved look that I remember all too well from the last time I chased him from my house.

Aldo Consoli smirks when my rounded eyes meet his.

"Get the fuck out of my house." My limbs are frozen in fear, but I force as much bravado into my voice as possible. Blood thunders against my eardrums, but it's not enough to drown out the music, its energetic beat suddenly as out of place as the shrill tunes of an ice cream truck driving past a funeral.

"Come on, now. You don't expect me to hear your little

party from the street and not come pay you a visit." He holds himself up against the wall, his wrinkled clothes disheveled and dirty.

I refuse to argue with him. No matter how loud I play my music, or how revealing my clothes, or how pleasant I act, I am not extending an invitation to invade my personal space. And no amount of arguing will justify that conclusion. "Get out. You have no right to be here."

I had thought my troubles with this man were over. Mom's debt had been paid. I'd assumed I was free of him and had even tucked Dad's pistol back where it belongs in his room. I couldn't have known Aldo would come back, but I berate myself regardless. How could I have been so careless?

Aldo raises himself upright off the wall with a lewd grin.

Sticky nausea fills my belly, curdling with fear and desperation. He's not going to leave. I know it in my gut. He's come back to take what he didn't get the first time, and if I can't find a way to escape, he's going to succeed.

I try not to be obvious as I consider what I can use as a weapon within reach.

"I stopped by to check on your little friend," he says, his speech slightly slurred. "But no one's home. When I heard your music and saw you dancing by yourself, I knew it was fate giving us a second chance." He steps toward the back of the sofa, inching closer to me.

I retreat, taking a wobbly step to the side, my calves pressed against the coffee table. I consider breaking my wineglass and using it as a weapon, but that seems so unreliable. What if I cut myself in the process? I need something heavy. A lamp. Or a fireplace poker. *Something.*

"She said her loan wasn't due for two more months." I don't care about the details of their deal. I just have to keep him talking so my frantic brain has a chance to figure a way out of this.

He shrugs. "Who's to say? There's nothing in writing."

*Fucking asshole.* I knew he'd pull something shady.

"If you touch me, my father will find out. You'll be crucified for hurting a family man's daughter."

The icy grin that splits his face is dripping with superiority. "I have permission to be here, and when you wanted to help work off a friend's debt, who's to say otherwise?"

Permission? Who else knew about Aldo's visits to Tuxedo Park? I try to peel apart his words, but before I can get the chance, he launches himself over the back of the couch. I spring toward the kitchen, hoping to make it to the back door, but searing pain lances through my scalp when he grabs my ponytail and yanks me backward.

My body ricochets off his. Before I can use the momentum to pull away, arms wrap like steel bands around me. I cry out, my throat burning with the effort, but it's pointless. The music is too loud for anyone to hear, even if we did have neighbors close enough to help me. I'm trapped in my own home with a deranged sociopath intent on raping me. His cock is already hard against my backside. The unwelcome feel of it makes me thrash viciously against his hold.

"That's it, little girl," Aldo hisses joyously. "Fight me. Make me want it." His caustic words grate against my ear, the moisture from his breath clinging to the skin of my neck.

I want to dip myself in acid to cleanse away the feel of him.

Bending forward as much as I can, I suddenly snap backward and slam my head into his nose.

"*Fuck!*" His curse booms over the music as he releases me momentarily.

I try to run again, but he grabs my hand and whips me around. Using my own momentum against me, he cracks his fist against my cheek, sending me stumbling to the ground.

The blaring music finally fades into the background while the world dips and weaves in slow motion. My thoughts are hazy and confused, but the fear never retreats. I know in every cell of my being that I'm in danger. That I have to move.

Blinking, I try to clear my thoughts. When I look behind me, I see Aldo assessing his bleeding nose in the living room mirror.

I did that.

He's trying to hurt me, and I busted his nose.

*I have to get out of here.*

"You little cunt. I think you broke my fucking nose."

Ignoring him, I pull myself up against the doorway into the kitchen. I have two options. I can make another attempt for the back door, or I can lunge for the block of cooking knives on the counter. I have only seconds to decide.

My left eye is quickly swelling, and my thoughts are frayed at the edges.

He may be drunk, but I'm no match for him in this state.

I'm not sure if it's resignation or determination or an overload of adrenaline, but an unnatural stillness settles over me as I lock eyes with my attacker.

Blue colliding with black.

Feral desperation warring with malicious psychosis.

Any debate about my next move becomes moot as I recognize that Aldo Consoli will never let me get away. Madness and alcohol have consumed him with the need to conquer me, and if I have any hope of escaping, it's in the form of an attack and not retreat.

I don't give him time to read my thoughts.

Lunging to the side, I dive into the kitchen and wrap my fingers around the handle of a knife just as he grabs my other hand and whips me around.

The next few seconds pass in a blur. As if time skips from one point to another.

First, I've got my hand outstretched to reach for the knife, and before I know how what's happened, I'm facing Aldo, his features contorted in astonishment as he looks down to where my knife is buried deep in his belly.

Point A to point B with no in-between.

We are both silent.

The world stills around us, all except for the damn music still blaring from the living room speakers. My eyes lift slowly to his. His seething hatred claws at my skin.

I need to get away, but I'm unwilling to part with my

weapon, so I yank back harshly, pulling the blade from his body and stumbling backward.

Aldo's lips round on a silent gasp, his hands quickly clutching at the growing wetness blossoming across his black shirt. The fabric is so dark that the stain doesn't even look like blood. But his shaking hand comes away crimson, and there's no denying the viscous substance dripping from my knife.

I don't think. I just run.

Out the back door. Knife in hand. Feet winged as I fly through the tall grass between my house and Hardwick.

It's late, so I go to the front of the house. The property is flooded with lights, enabling me to glance back and check that I wasn't followed. I bang on the door and ring the bell before doubling over, my lungs screaming with exertion.

I have to ring the bell a second time before Elena's rattled voice comes over the intercom.

"Can I help you?"

I look up toward the camera in the corner. "Elena, it's me, Luisa. There was a man at my house, and I may have killed him. I don't know. Please, I need your help." My voice is shrill and shaky. And as if hearing the trauma in my own voice makes it that much more real, all the muscles in my body begin to quiver and quake.

The locks quickly turn, and Elena flings open the door to usher me inside.

"Oh, God. Sweet girl, are you okay?" She secures the door behind me then wraps a comforting arm around my shoulders.

The hand still gripping the knife lifts before us, trembling. "I didn't know what else to do. He was going to hurt me. And ... and I grabbed the knife, and then it was in him. I don't even know how."

Elena moves in front of me to gain my attention. "Stay right here for just a second. I'm coming right back, okay?"

I nod.

She's only gone for a handful of seconds, but in that time, my chest begins to shake with the threat of sobs. Elena wraps a hand towel around my fist, coaxing my fingers to release their grip. She rolls the knife into the towel and sets it on a table.

"Let's get you upstairs and cleaned up."

She takes my hand in hers and leads me to the nearest guest bedroom. I follow in a haze. My brain is so overwhelmed with shock, I can't manage even basic thoughts. While Elena starts a hot shower in the on-suite bathroom, I stare blankly at the wall.

Then her eyes are in front of me, blue pools of worry.

She places her gentle hands on my cheeks. "I know you're scared, sweet Luisa, but everything is going to be okay. You shower and try to calm down."

I nod because that's what I'm supposed to do.

"I'll be right outside the door if you need me. We'll take care of everything, sweet girl, I promise."

Once she slips from the room, I dazedly remove my blood-spattered clothes. I can't look at them. The fabric is discarded into a pile on the floor. The heat of the shower spray warms my skin, but it can't touch the permafrost coating my bones. When I lift my hands to the water, I see the blood staining my fingers. Under the nails. Blotching my skin. Filling each crease and crevice.

My shaking amplifies until I have to sink to the shower floor.

What have I done? Did I just kill a man? If he isn't dead, will he come after me? What about my family? Would he report me to the police? The Mafia usually doesn't involve the cops, but if he takes himself to a hospital, they might report the incident.

If he's alive.

If he's not, will I be in trouble with the Giordano family? The law would deem my actions self-defense, but would the Mafia be so understanding?

I had to do what I did. I don't regret it, but what consequences will it bring?

The uncertainty is terrifying.

Reaching for the bar of soap, I scrub at my skin as sobs wrack my body. I try to stay quiet. I'm not even sure why. Maybe because a part of me still feels unsafe. As though my cries will alert the world to what I've done.

I scour my flesh until I can't tell if I'm red from blood stains or excessive scrubbing. Eventually, I force myself to turn off the water. Silence awaits me. I used to love time alone—time for my mind to be free—but now, the silence is a petri dish for toxic thoughts and fears.

As I towel off, a soft knock sounds on the door. "Luisa, dear, I've got a change of clothes for you. Can I come in?"

I open the door and accept the stack of clothes she offers. "Thank you," I whisper hoarsely, my throat raw from crying.

"Of course. I've got a small tray of food along with some juice out here on the vanity. Help yourself. It might calm your nerves. Will you be okay up here tonight? I can stay in the room next door if you're more comfortable having someone close."

The world doesn't deserve Elena De Rossi. Her kindness and generosity are without reproach, and I have a sudden epiphany that a woman like her wouldn't stray from her husband except in the most desperate of circumstances. If she found companionship in the arms of my father, it was for a good reason. Zeno may idolize his father, but I would bet money his parents' marriage wasn't what he thought. That Silvano De Rossi wasn't who Zeno thought he was.

"Thank you so much, Elena. I'll be fine up here until I can sort things in the morning." In the light of day, once the monsters are gone.

"You're always welcome here. We'll get this all sorted tomorrow, I promise. For now, you take care of yourself. Get some rest and know that you're safe at Hardwick." She pulls me in for a motherly hug despite the stray droplets of water dotting my skin.

I cling to her and the assurances she offers. I've handled my own problems for a long time. I had to. My mother wasn't the type of mom I could turn to for help. Dad was always there for me, but there's something different about a mother's love. A generosity that I never experienced. Elena isn't my mother, but at this moment, her maternal love for me is unquestionable.

When I pull back, emotions lodge in my throat. I can't

speak, but I hope she can see the gratitude and love I have for her through my tear-filled eyes.

Once she leaves, I put on the clothes she provided and slip beneath the covers of the king-sized bed. I leave the light on in the bathroom. I'm not ready to face the dark and the images it will summon. I would play music if I had my phone, but it got left behind at the cottage. There is nothing in the stately room to distract my mind save for the intricate chandelier above me. I start at the top and count the crystals, dull in the dim lighting. There are three hundred and twenty-five. I make it to one-hundred and thirty-two on my third count before exhaustion finally pulls me under.

# CHAPTER 6

I haven't been asleep long when I wake, curled into a ball in the middle of the bed. I don't know why I've woken until I sense a presence in the room. Terror floods my veins in an instant, but when I jerk upright, it's Zeno I see sitting in the corner of the room.

He lifts his hand to calm me. "It's okay, Isa. It's just me." The gentle purr of his voice instantly soothes my thundering pulse back from near cardiac arrest.

"Z." It's the only word I can squeeze past my constricting throat, but it's all he needs to hear. Every bit of my fear and vulnerability is there in that one syllable. Zeno came when I needed him most, and my relief is instantaneous.

He swiftly rises from his chair and joins me on the bed. I crawl onto his lap without hesitation, my body trembling from the comfort of his arms wrapping securely around me, as though I'd been holding in my fear and anxiety coiled tight in each muscle while I slept, but the presence of this mercurial man is all I need to release that tension.

"Jesus, you had me worried," he murmurs into my hair. "I've never driven so fast in my life."

His admission makes me recall that he was in the Hamptons this weekend. That's a three-and-a-half-hour drive. Assuming Elena called him, he must have jumped in his car before he even hung up the phone.

"I'd say I'm sorry to pull you away from work, but I'm not," I whisper.

Z gently eases back, coaxing me to lift my face toward his. When I do, his eyes dilate with murderous intent as he examines my bruised cheek. I'd been too tucked away beneath the covers for him to see before, but with the bathroom light still on, my discolored cheek is now visible. His fingertips raise to trace a delicate circle around the outer edge of my swelling.

His touch is reverent. An apology and a promise.

Never again.

"I need you to tell me every way he hurt you." His eyes light with pain, and I realize what he's asking.

I shake my head. "He didn't touch me like that. He wanted to, but I got away before he could."

Zeno's chest expands with air, but his features never soften. His relief will not grant Aldo any leniency, should the man still be alive.

At that moment, I feel the full impact of what I mean to Zeno De Rossi.

Every caustic comment and brutal rebuff from the past melt away as concrete understanding settles in my bones. He would slaughter the city for me. Raise the dead and give his own life for me. The enormity of his feelings is there in his eyes, waiting to be seen. Waiting for me to look hard enough to see the truth.

I am the center of Zeno's world. Always have been. Always will be.

I don't need to understand the man to know that one simple truth.

My lips beg for his touch. I readjust until I'm straddling his lap, my eyes never leaving his. His strong arms hold me against him with one hand firmly at the back of my neck. Once we're face-to-face, I rest my forehead gently against his.

Zeno's body is stiff with uncertainty and restraint. For once, I don't presume to know his reasons. It's not my place to project my own interpretations. Instead, I bring my lips to his hesitantly and allow fate to take us where it will.

My lungs steal his shuddered breath before his mouth seizes mine.

A primal moan rattles his chest and buries itself deep in my heart. Our tongues taste one another with the urgency of starvation. Years of deprivation and need are released all at once. Barriers drop, and bridles rip free. For the first time in our adult lives, we give ourselves over to the connection that has always lived and breathed between us. Nothing else exists. No families or duties. No past or future. We are two people fully engaged in our present need for one another.

"Fuck, I don't deserve this." His hand kneads my ass cheek while his teeth graze against my bottom lip.

"No talking about the past." I shake my head. "We can deal with it later. Right now, we need this. *I* need this."

"Tell me exactly what you need because I want to fuck you. If that's not what you mean, say it now." His words are ragged, taut with restraint.

"That's exactly what I want. I need to feel you inside me."

Without another word, Zeno rolls our bodies back onto the mattress until he's looming over me. Possessive yet tender, ardent desire burning in his eyes. Our hips align, and my knees raise to align my center fully against his hard length. The relief from his touch where I most need him steals the air from my lungs.

His kiss is savage. Feral in its intensity but absolute in its reverence. He makes me feel cherished with the simplest touch, and I devour every delectable bite.

Eventually, Zeno lifts himself long enough to remove his shirt, then slips mine up over my head. I want to study every inch of him, worship and memorize his breathtaking body, but he doesn't give me the opportunity. Consumed with his own ravaging desires, he descends to the column of my neck, trailing kisses down to my chest. I wasn't wearing my bra when I'd gone to bed, so I'm bare to him. My body as naked as my emotions, raw and exposed and utterly his in every way.

While he showers my breasts with attention, I drift my

hands over his broad shoulders. The muscles flex and coil beneath my fingers. He's so solid. So strong and masculine. Yet I've never felt so safe with a man. As if his strength is an extension of my own. His body mine to command.

I cry out when his teeth tug at my nipple. The jolt is the perfect marriage of pleasure and pain. Zeno makes my body sing with desire until my core weeps, and a sheen of perspiration coats my skin.

"How many times have I dreamed of tasting you? Hundreds. Thousands." His body lowers until his head is positioned at the apex of my thighs. Eyes locked on mine, his tongue takes a slow, languorous lick along my slit. "Not once did my imagination live up to this. You're fucking *divine*."

I moan his name as he devours me. Fingers kneading at my breast, tongue relentlessly circling my swollen bundle of nerves, Zeno unravels the fabric of my being. I am nothing but pleasure and writhing greed, relentlessly chasing that perfect moment of carnal bliss.

When his finger slips past my entrance and finds its way to that perfect spot inside me, I don't have to chase anything. Release crashes over me like the torrential downpour of a summer storm. My throat burns from a scream I can't hear. I'm too lost in the liquid elation coursing through the highways and byways of my body. He coaxes every possible shudder and shiver from my body like an artist crafting the perfect portrait.

"*Zeno*." I breathe his name to remind myself that this is real. He's here, and for the moment, he's mine.

The loss of his touch draws open my eyes. I watch

raptly as he unbuttons his pants and allows them to pool on the floor. His naked, tattooed form is on full display, and I have never laid eyes on anything so flawless. Models and actors are sculpted with muscle, but Zeno's body is more than an aesthetic. He is the embodiment of power and strength, and I have no doubt he knows how to wield both.

He rolls on a condom, and I'm not sure what's more erotic: his straining cock, or his broad hand fisting that hard length. His abs ripple with his movements, and I feel each twitch of his muscles deep in my belly. I know it's safer to use protection, so I don't object, but damn if I don't crave the unobstructed feel of him. I'm tired of things coming between us. Even the thin rubber barrier is a burden after so many years of conflict and strain.

But we aren't there yet. For now, I'll savor what I can.

When his body aligns with mine, my breaths become shallow with anticipation. The scalding heat of his cock radiates through the condom and soothes my aching clit, but only for a second. With one arch of his hips, he's at my entrance, pressing inside me. Once, twice, three thrusts find him fully sheathed within me. My jaw drops at the fullness, and my eyes stray up toward the ceiling.

"*Eyes on me, Isa.*" Strain tugs at Zeno's voice. A vein bulges in his neck, and his triceps bunch with effort.

I do as he says, and only when our gazes are locked does he resume his movements. One quick thrust, then a slow retreat before surging back inside me. He speaks a million words in those ocean eyes of his, but there's only one I hear. One word can be discerned without interpretation.

*Mine.*

I respond in kind with the only thing left for me to say.

*Yours.*

Zeno rewards me with an increase in his pace, pounding into me with the intensity of a holy man seeking God. My core is still sensitive from release, each of his movements re-igniting the fire in my belly. I move my body in tandem with his. A push and pull as natural as waves crashing on the shore. Over and over, we melt together in pleasure.

My body is alight with sensation, but when Zeno finds his release inside me, it's my heart that seizes with feeling. Emotions threaten to overwhelm me. To consume and destroy me. Being with Zeno is something I've only ever let myself imagine in my darkest moments. Times of great weakness when I sacrificed my pride to give my heart a taste of the impossible.

Or so I thought.

I never believed something like this could happen, but it has, and I've never experienced sex bound with such intense emotion. All my past escapades shrivel and pale in light of what exists between Zeno and me.

He clutches me tight, my name wrenched from his lips, over and over, his cock pulsing deep within me. Once his movements still, he brings his lips to mine one last time in a kiss fraught with tenderness and devotion. He then slips away to the bathroom. This is his house, so I wonder for the briefest second if he'll leave now to go to his own room, but that thought is banished when he joins me back in bed. He spoons his body around mine, pulling me against him with a strong arm around my middle. We lie on our sides, bodies molded together, lungs expanding and contracting in sync with one another.

I trail my fingers absently over the ridges of his knuckles, not wanting to move and burst the bubble keeping us safe from reality. I note the dusting of hair on the back of his hand and a few smooth slivers of skin that I attribute to scar tissue. There is something alluring about a man's hands—the embodiment of masculinity and physical strength. They are a roadmap of a person's aptitudes and experiences, and Zeno's hands reveal that he's no stranger to hard work.

"I don't want to upset you by forcing the subject," Zeno says softly. "But I need to know what happened. Did you recognize the man who broke in?"

I breathe deeply through my nose. My mother's problems can no longer be kept a secret. I'm not sure how Z will respond to the truth, but I have to tell him.

"The reason I had to move back home is because I discovered that my mom has been gambling, and she got herself into debt with a family bookie. I knew what that would mean for Dad, so I used my school savings to pay off her debt. After, I told my dad what was going on. He was pissed, but I knew he didn't have the money to handle the matter himself, and there was no way in hell I was letting the family label him a deadbeat and possibly hurt him."

Z is silent for several seconds as he absorbs the information. "I would tell you that you should have come to me, but I understand why you didn't. I'm fucking pissed at myself, though. You should never have been in that situation."

I squeeze his hand, holding his arm tight against my chest to let him know I appreciate his remorse. "None of it was a problem until the bookie came to the house drunk one day while everyone else was gone."

Zeno's body goes inhumanly still. "This has happened more than once?" His guttural words are infused with lethal calm.

"Not as bad," I whisper. "But, yeah. I was able to escape and get one of my dad's guns."

"Jesus *Christ!*" Z rolls away from me and surges from the bed, a hand stabbing through his hair as he paces back and forth before turning a wall of fury in my direction. "His name." The two clipped words hiss between clenched teeth.

"Aldo Consoli." My voice is small. I know Z isn't mad at me, and I'm certain he'd never hurt me, but I've never witnessed this side of him. Not to this extent. He is the embodiment of righteous vengeance. If anything, I'm scared for anyone who stumbles into his path.

Z grabs his clothes and begins to hastily redress.

"What are you doing?" I blurt.

"I have to go. This is all my fault, and I need to fix it."

"*Stop.*" My command is strong enough to snag his attention. "You haven't slept, and there's nothing that can be done at three in the morning. Please, stay until the sun is up so I don't spend the rest of the night worrying."

His piercing stare holds firm, but I know I've won when

the tension in his shoulders eases. Slowly, he strips his clothes back off and returns to the bed. This time, he lies on his back and pulls me into his side. His body is still, but the press of my ear to his chest reveals a thundering pulse.

"Tell me the rest," he instructs with a forced calm.

"I got him paid off, but when he came to collect the money, Grace happened to come by our house to get her mom's sewing scissors. The two talked, and when Grace heard that Aldo had loaned Mom money, she decided borrowing from him would help get her moved to the city sooner rather than later. When I learned what she'd done, I was terrified. I tried to get her to return the money and back out, but she refused. I've been so worried for her, but I didn't think I personally had anything to worry about anymore. Last night, I was listening to music, and I guess he heard it on his way to pay a visit to Grace. I guess that's what he does—get drunk, then seek out female customers to offer discounts for ... services. That or change the terms of his loans to coerce an *exchange*. I hate him with every fiber of my being."

"How did he get inside the house?"

"I don't know exactly. The music was loud, and he was suddenly there. I tried to get away, and we fought. That's how I got this." I motion to my cheek. "Then he was so angry, I knew I'd never get away. That I had to find a weapon." My voice begins to quiver.

Zeno's arm holds me tighter against him while his other hand cradles my head. "You don't have to say any more," he whispers. "I'm so proud of you, Isa. You did exactly as you should have, and I'll take care of everything else. I promise."

I nod and try to take a calming breath. "There's something else you should know about last night," I tell him. "When I threatened Aldo with the probability that he'd get in trouble for hurting me, he said he had permission to be here in the Park. I never saw him drive a car, so as far as I know, he could have been climbing the wall to get in. He could have been lying, but I figure you should know."

Zeno trails his fingers through my hair. "No permission will exonerate him from what he's done. Coming onto my fucking property to hurt anyone on my estate. As I said, you don't need to worry about any of it again. I'm here, and for now, all you need to do is get some rest."

"Okay."

My head still rests above his heart. I don't expect to sleep, considering everything that's happened, but nestled safely against Z's warm body, lulled by his gentle caress, my thoughts drift to unconsciousness. I slip into a deep, cathartic sleep and don't wake again until the sun is well into the sky.

When I come to, I don't have one of those moments when everything comes rushing back to me in a flash of memory. Between the pulsing pain in my left cheekbone and Zeno's scent blanketed around me, my conscious mind is all too aware of all that's happened in the past twelve hours. Even the fact that I'm now alone in the bed doesn't come as a surprise. Considering how urgently Z wanted to start his manhunt, I doubt he waited five minutes after I'd fallen asleep to leave.

I sit up and scan the room around me, unsure what to do next. Do I go home? Is Aldo dead on my kitchen floor?

*Did I kill a man last night?*

The possibilities make me want to retreat beneath the covers and never leave this room. I have so many questions, but that one worries me the most. I'm desperate to know the answer but equally terrified. I don't want to have killed anyone, but I also hate to think of Aldo alive and hungry for my blood. Regardless of my aversion, I have to know.

If he did survive, could he be at the house waiting for my return? Surely, his need for vengeance wouldn't overrule his need to save himself and get medical attention. I can safely assume that Z has stopped by the cottage to assess things for himself, but I'm not going over until I know for sure. That's when I notice my phone on the nightstand. I left it at the house when I ran. Zeno must have brought my phone back after checking out the scene.

I could call and ask Z what he found at my house, but he won't want to discuss it over the phone. If he came back to Hardwick with my phone, he might still be here. My best bet for answers is to go in search of him and hope he hasn't left.

I'm up and dressed in an instant. Aside from my need to know what's going on, my family will be back from the city anytime. I don't have the luxury of burying my head in the sand. I've got to get home and clean the blood out of the kitchen. I'm not sure why, but I don't want them to know what happened. I don't want them to see our family home the way I am now feeling about it. Unsafe. Tainted.

While I'm in the bathroom, I examine the bruise on my cheek. It doesn't look as bad as I expected, but there will be no hiding it from my family. I'll have to decide what I'm willing to tell them. Maybe once I know more myself, the answer will come to me.

When I reach the bottom of the stairs, Elena is sipping coffee in the sitting area right off the main entry. Her face lights up when our gazes meet.

"Isa," she says my name with relieved affection and hurries over. "Were you able to get some sleep?"

"Yes, thank you." I glance in the direction of Zeno's office. "Is Z still here?"

"No, but he did let me know on his way out that you were safe to go home, if that's what you want. Of course, you're welcome to stay here as well."

Safe to go home—what does that mean? Was Aldo dead? Surely not, or Zeno would have come to tell me himself, right? Is he out dealing with my attack, or is his disappearance part of an awkward morning after? I have no idea where our night leaves us. Will he text me on his own? Am I supposed to reach out? If he told his mom to pass along a message, I should probably assume that's the extent of what he needs to say at the moment. It's not particularly informative, but it's at least something to go on.

I smile and nod. "That's good to hear. I ought to get back before my family gets home."

"Would you like a cup of coffee before you go?"

"If I can take it to go, then sure. But I really need to get going."

She places a gentle hand on my arm. "Of course, let me get you a travel mug."

I follow her back to the kitchen, where she loads me up with a ton of coffee, and I give her a hearty thanks before slipping out the back exit. I've been given the all clear to return home, but even in the bright light of day, my nerves have me searching the shadows for hidden dangers. Elena offered to walk with me, but my silly pride insisted I'd be fine.

I would pick up my pace to a healthy stroll if I wasn't somewhat dreading what I'd find at the house. I'm not in an outright panic because Zeno wouldn't have told me the place was safe if it wasn't. When I reach the back door, I find it unlocked. Slowly, I ease open the door. My eyes immediately cut to the block of knives on the counter across the room. Every slot is filled. Each knife handle is in place.

Confused, I tiptoe around the small island to discover the floor on the other side is immaculate. There's not a drop of blood. No sign of a struggle at all.

I'm stunned. The incident already feels like a living nightmare. To see my kitchen looking as though nothing ever happened is surreal. If I didn't know better, I'd say Aldo's attack had never even happened, but the sticky memories I can't escape are too real to be a product of my imagination.

I walk around the corner to the living room. Everything looks to be in order, but when I place my hand on the carpet where my glass of wine spilled, the area is wet.

Either Zeno cleaned the place himself, or he had someone else do it. That is the only explanation.

I have to know what happened—what Z found when he arrived at the house. I have to know if I killed Aldo Consoli. I don't have the patience to worry about upsetting Z by calling. I don't care about dating protocols or anything else. I need answers.

I open my phone and dial his number.

"Everything okay?" Zeno answers his phone with an urgency to his voice.

"Yes, everything's fine. I just got over to my parents' house. Z, I need to know if I ... k—"

Before I can say more, he cuts me off. "Not over the phone, Isa. I'll be back later today. We can talk in person."

"Oh, yeah. Okay." My eyes scrunch shut in annoyance at myself. Of course, I shouldn't be saying something incriminating over the phone. "Just answer one question. Was there anyone here when you got here?"

"No."

The sound echoes in my ears. The word bears such finality, but in this case, it births a world of uncertainty. Aldo left the house alive, but what happened after? Where is he now? Will he come after me?

"Alright, then," I respond, my voice thin and reed-like. "Well, thank you, again, for your help."

"Isa," Zeno calls to me, his voice a gentle caress. "I told you I'll handle it. He won't touch you again, understand?"

"Yeah, okay," I whisper.

"I'll see you soon, sweet girl." His murmured words melt my heart like warm butter.

"Bye, Z." I end the call and breathe deeply.

I don't want to panic about Aldo, so I give myself over to thoughts of Z instead. I'd rather overthink that situation than dwell on the possible dangers around me.

After so many years at odds with him, having Z back in my life feels like a dream. A glorious, intoxicating, ethereal dream. It's hard for me to comprehend that it's happening. I suppose the real test will come when I see him again. Will I sense cool restraint in his presence, or will he seal his place in my heart? I didn't get the sense last night that Zeno's interest in me had been transient, but our history makes it hard to wash away the uncertainty. Enough uncertainty that I have plenty to contemplate until my family shows up a half hour later.

They parade through the front door like any other day but stop short when they get a glimpse of my face. The only one who doesn't gape and pepper me with questions is my father. He doesn't say a single word. Not out loud. But his remorseful stare speaks volumes.

Zeno has informed him of the situation. It's the only explanation.

I have no doubt my father now knows all about Aldo. It's there in the murderous cut to his jaw and slow intervals of his measured breaths. He's a powder keg of emotions waiting to ignite.

I assure everyone that my injury was a product of my own doing—too much wine at my impromptu dance party and a sneaky coffee table wanting in on the action. I point out the wet carpet as evidence of my shenanigans and breathe a sigh of relief when Mom and my sisters accept my excuse as the truth. Mom chatters airily about their outings with my aunt while Livia rolls her eyes and charges upstairs without saying hello. For once, I encourage Mom's incessant blathering with feigned interest until I notice the effervescent smile on Gia's face. It hasn't faded an ounce since she walked in the door, aside from a few moments of concern over my black eye.

When she slips upstairs to unpack, I sneak away from Mom to follow her. "You sure look happy to be home," I say once we're alone in our room.

The joy shining in her eyes warms my chest.

"Carter reached out yesterday. I thought about calling you but decided to wait and tell you in person. He and the kids will be back today and have invited all of us over to celebrate Zeno's birthday this evening. He was so sweet, Isa. I don't know what all happened in the last couple of weeks, but I think he may have sorted his feelings. I'm just so happy he's coming back." A healthy flush has returned to her porcelain skin, and I'm reassured that her heart is well on its way to full repair.

A tidal swell of relief makes my sinuses burn with the threat of tears. "Oh, Gia. I'm so thrilled for you." I pull my sister into a hug, and when we pull away from one another, her eyes are glassy.

"Who knows what will happen. I'm just glad there's a chance. I missed him and the kids so much."

"I know you did, honey."

Did Zeno play a role in Carter's return? If he did, he took the initiative before our night together. He'd listened to my perspective when we spoke, that I can say for certain. I don't know for sure whether he took corrective action, but my gut insists that he did. That all his barriers between us have dropped, and it's changing him.

He's changing me, too. Making me realize how quick I've been to jump to conclusions. There are so many things in this world that I know nothing about. How incredibly brazen I've been to judge what I don't know.

"We're supposed to go over for dinner at six. I thought I'd make cookies to take with us. I'm sure Mrs. Larson will have a cake, but the kids love iced sugar cookies."

"I'm sure they'd appreciate that." I grin, so incredibly happy for my sister.

I debate telling her about Zeno and me, but I'm not sure what to say. I don't want to scare her about Aldo, and otherwise, it's a bit odd to explain how Z and I came together. Plus, I want to see him in person and put to rest the last of my fears before I go professing my feelings for him. If there's any chance he's going to regret sleeping with me, that should be obvious by this evening once he's had plenty of time to consider what he's done. Until then, I'll wait anxiously to learn my future.

# CHAPTER 7

Dad insists we drive to the Bishops' rather than walk. No one argues, but my mother gives him an odd look, and I understand why. The evening is unusually temperate. Dad loves the outdoors and would normally be the first to suggest we all walk and take full advantage of the weather. It's out of character, but no one says anything. I suspect he has finally decided to err on the side of caution in light of recent events.

Livia has gone to a friend's house, leaving Gia, Marca, and me in the back seat of the car, along with Gia's tray of cookies. Zeno and Elena are already at the house when we arrive. My insides twist and flutter at the sight of him, unable to decide if they are more nervous or excited.

I'd completely forgotten about his birthday. I feel bad not having a gift or even a card, but we were hardly even speaking to one another a week ago. So much has changed in such a short span of time.

He and Elena join Carter at the door to welcome us. I pay special attention to Zeno's interaction with my father. Dad is stiff and reserved, adding to my suspicions that the two have spoken recently. I wonder what was said and desperately hope Zeno isn't angry with my father. Dad's discomfort seems to be one-sided, which makes me think any blame he's feeling is likely self-imposed.

My mother croons when Z places a welcoming kiss on her cheek. He is surprisingly attentive to her and even gives Marca a special hello when he normally sticks to a stoic nod or a raised glass in lieu of a greeting. When it's my turn to pass before him at the tail end of our little procession, his eyes soften as his fingers weave through my hair to cup the back of my head. He pulls me close to place a kiss on my forehead as though it's a ritual gesture we share frequently.

I momentarily forget how to breathe.

Gia pauses from her cheerful reunion with Carter to shoot me a bulging stare. I give her an innocent shrug as Carter's two kids come rushing in. They wrap Gia in hugs and excitedly survey the cookies she made. The foursome is a Hallmark movie come to life, and I can't help but grin at their happiness. Curious at its origin, I glance back at Zeno with a questioning look, but he merely raises a single quizzical brow and ushers me forward with a hand at the small of my back.

As we walk toward the living area, I realize Cora is nowhere to be seen. It doesn't necessarily mean anything, but one can only hope her absence is permanent. Even if she wasn't solely responsible for Carter's hasty exit, her snobby attitude couldn't have helped.

Without Cora's snide comments or Livia's whining, our gathering is perfectly crafted for the lighthearted enjoyment of a summer evening. Carter grills burgers. Gia and Marca play a card game with Boston and Emily. I sip on a Michelob Ultra and try not to stare at Z while he chats with Carter by the grill. It's a storybook evening, aside from being asked several times what happened to my eye. I'd prefer not to be reminded of the homicidal lunatic who tried to rape me but cannot escape the questions about something as noticeable as a shiner. I pass along the same made-up story I'd told my family, and no one raises any doubts. They laugh along with me as I regale my clumsiness, and the subject moves on to safer waters.

Not long after we finish eating, Zeno steps into the yard to take a quick phone call. When he returns, he's all business. Every ounce of birthday levity from minutes before has been erased.

"Carter, I hate to do this, but I've been called to the city on urgent business."

"Oh ... well, I hope everything is all right."

"Yeah, but I have to head out earlier than I would have liked." Zeno's eyes slide briefly to mine.

"You want us to package up a slice of cake for you? I'd hate for you to miss your own birthday cake."

"How about you send a piece home with my mother? Antonio, would you mind giving her a ride back to Hardwick?"

Dad nods gravely. "Of course. I'll make sure she gets home safely."

"I appreciate that," Zeno says, turning his attention back to Carter. "And sorry again to run. We'll have to return the favor at my place next."

"Absolutely. Be safe on your way out."

Z smiles and nods his appreciation at a chorus of happy birthdays before making a hasty exit inside the house. I can't let him leave without knowing if the call was about Aldo. I jump up with a muttered, "Excuse me," and dash for the back door.

"Z, wait!" I call out through the house as the front door clicks shut. When I reach the door and fling it open, I'm able to flag him down before he's in his car. "Wait! I need to talk to you, just for a minute."

He closes the car door, and in several long strides, meets me on the other side of the black Range Rover. "I need to get going, Isa."

"I know, but the uncertainty is killing me. You have to tell me what's going on. Do you know where Aldo went? Is he still alive?" *Will he come after me?*

Flyaway hairs pull free from my messy bun when the evening breeze blows past. Zeno's fingers coax them back behind my ears, then trail down to cup either side of my neck. His thumbs on my jaw angle my chin up to receive his kiss. A sensual caress filled with assurance, apology, and promise.

"The less you know, the better, but be assured that I'm handling it." His voice is as coarse as the gravel at our feet. He turns his head to the side and lets out a sharp whistle that startles me but not as much as seeing two men materialize from the bushes not twenty feet from us.

I instinctively reach for Zeno. "What the hell?"

"Easy, Isa. They're with me. I wanted you to know that I've had eyes on you since the moment you left my house this morning. You have nothing to worry about."

"Is Aldo the reason you're leaving?" I can't help but push for more. I want to know what's happening.

He takes a slow step back without offering an answer, spoken or otherwise. When he takes a second step and starts to turn away, I call out one last question. He may be adamant about refusing to discuss Aldo, but there's one topic he can't deny me.

"What is this, Z? What's happening with us?"

He pauses, his inscrutable gaze coming back to mine. "This is whatever you want it to be. I've told you how I feel—it's been the same since we were teens. What comes next is up to you."

His admission winds me. Baffles and bemuses me.

I don't say another word as he slips into his car and disappears into the night. I am speechless. A part of me genuinely expected him to be distant this evening and show some sign of second thoughts, but that couldn't be farther from the truth. Zeno De Rossi cares for me. He still wants me, despite the horrific things I said. The insults. The accusations.

And if I'm honest with myself, I want him too.

It's like Gia said weeks ago. Some people we simply never get over—no matter the time or distance that spans between us. That has always been Zeno for me. It's the reason his insults continued to hurt, and it was my motivation for never giving up on him.

Z is that one person who will always live in my heart and own a piece of my soul.

I never dared to dream the opposite might be true—that I might be that person for him as well. Who am I to reject that kind of divine connection? I couldn't even if I wanted to. And I don't. Even now, I'm anxious for him to return. Now that I've had a taste of what we could share, I'm ravenous for more.

I take a lungful of the mild, humid air to ground myself.

The sentries Zeno summoned have sunken back into the shadows and are no longer visible. I appreciate knowing they are watching, but their invisibility is an unsettling reminder of how easy it would be for an enemy to approach unseen. I hurry back inside, locking the door behind me, and wind my way to the back of the house, where I happen to spot Carter in the kitchen. When I step closer, I discover he's alone and decide to seize the opportunity.

"Hey, Carter. Do you have a minute to chat?"

He whips around from the fridge, a bottle of water in hand. "Sure! I was just grabbing some water. Want a bottle?"

"No, thanks. I'm good."

He closes the door and strolls toward me. "What can I help you with?"

"I wanted to talk to you about Gia," I say softly. Both because it's a sensitive subject and because I don't want to be overheard.

His lips thin, and his blond eyebrows knot together. "Is she okay?"

"She is now, but your stint in the city was hard on her. I would normally never butt into someone's life like this, but this is important. Gia isn't like most people. She keeps her emotions guarded, so it can be hard to tell what she's feeling. I want you to know that she adores you and the kids. If there is any doubt in your mind, please know that it's unfounded. I've never seen her so happy as when she learned you were returning." Lord forgive me, but it needed to be said. If I leave it up to Gia, Carter might never feel confident enough in her affection to pursue her.

Carter toys with the lid on his water bottle, eyes cast downward. "She's come to mean a great deal to us. The last few weeks weren't easy on me either, and we won't be leaving again anytime soon." When his eyes lift to mine, they glow with love and conviction.

I give his forearm a gentle squeeze. "That's so wonderful to hear. I guess we better get back outside before they devour the cake without us."

"They wouldn't dare." He gives me a scandalous look.

"Wouldn't they?" I tease back.

We start for the back patio, and I can't help but dig for information on his sister. "Did Cora decide to stay in the city a while longer?"

"We decided it was best for everyone if she spent a little less time here." He glances back at me with a cryptic glint in his eye.

"Ah, well. They say absence makes the heart grow fonder."

"Indeed." Carter opens the glass patio door and motions for me to go first with a smirk.

The rest of our night passes without further disruption. Dad takes Elena home before coming back to chauffeur us to the cottage.

"Liv texted that she's back home," Mom informs no one in particular. "She said she was going to bed early because she wasn't feeling well. Hopefully, she hasn't picked up a stomach bug. We'll all end up with it."

Dad parks out front of the house, ignoring Mom's comment. "Isa, why don't you come around to the front for a minute. I'd like to have a private word."

Mom, Gia, and Marca all turn to stare at me. I widen my eyes with a look that says, "What? You know as much as me," then exit the back seat. Talks with my dad are rarely heavy, so it's easy to make like of his request in front of the others, but on the inside, I know this talk will be different. This isn't our normal subject matter, and I can sense how upset he is.

Once we're alone, the car becomes saturated with tension. It radiates from my father like heat from a flame, and I begin to realize how much he's been holding back since they returned home. Since he learned what his willful ignorance has enabled.

"Did Zeno call you?" I ask quietly.

"He did. First thing this morning. He told me what happened last night. You can't imagine how upset I was." Dad pauses, his eyes unseeing out the front windshield. "But when ... when he informed me that it wasn't the first time Aldo had gone after you, I thought my skin would blister my anger burned so bad. At myself and Aldo, but also you." His words are brutally honest and spoken with painstaking calm. They slowly drive a stake into my heart and wrench my chest wide open.

My lips part to speak, but no sound emerges. Emotion squeezes down on my throat.

"Do you have any idea what it's like to find out my baby was—" his words catch, and he has to take a deep breath before continuing. "My baby was *attacked* right in our own home, and she didn't trust me enough to tell me? To let me know so I could make sure it didn't happen again?" Dad clenches the steering wheel in both hands, his knuckles bleeding to white. "I know none of it was your fault and that you're innocent in all this. I'm not trying to blame you. I just always thought that of my four girls, you'd be the one who would trust me with anything. Yet, somehow, I fucked up enough that even my Lulu thought she had to take on a monster by herself."

Tears tumble down my cheeks as I watch my daddy's chin quiver with regret.

Regardless of what he said at the start, he's not mad at me. He's furious with himself. But as much as I hate for him to be upset, there's a part of me realizing for the first time that he's right. I don't fully trust him, and that breaks my heart even more than witnessing his self-loathing.

Where Aldo is concerned, I had a variety of reasons for not speaking up about his first assault attempt that didn't necessarily involve my father. But in addition, I was also reluctant to go to my father with my problems because he can be dismissive that any real trouble exists. How many times have I gone to him with concerns about Mom and my sisters? And how many excuses has he made on their behalf? I adore my father, but he isn't a man of action. As much as it hurts to admit, Dad is just as flawed as any other person, no matter how much I've idolized him.

"Why don't you ever confront her?" I ask with a shaky breath. If we're going to talk about what happened, we're going to address the cause, not the result. Mom has been dragging our family down for years while Dad stands by and turns a blind eye. If we're going to talk about trust, then we'll go straight to the root of the matter.

"Because I didn't realize how destructive she'd become."

"You didn't want to see it, and I can understand that. I adore you, Daddy, always have and always will, but we needed you to step in and be the parent Mom couldn't be. Marca *still* needs that." I try to speak with tenderness because I know what I'm saying has to hurt. Confronting his shortcomings isn't easy, but that's one area where he's better than most. Dad's not afraid to be wrong.

He turns his bloodshot eyes in my direction. "I'm so sorry, baby girl. I just ... I never thought..."

I lean forward swiftly and wrap my arms around him, assuring him of my love. "It's okay, Daddy. I know you never meant anything bad to happen."

His body hitches with a shuddered breath that matches my own, and his arms clutch me tightly. As tough as it is to have such a difficult conversation and to see my father so distraught, I'm relieved it happened. That I voiced the things needing to be said, and that for once, Dad heard me.

He pulls back eventually, after we've both settled, and

wipes at his eyes. "I want you to know things are going to change. *I'm* going to change."

"As long as you're still you," I say softly. "You mean the world to me, Daddy, just as you are."

He gives me a sad smile and kisses my cheek. "Enough with the waterworks. Let's get inside."

I'm happy to oblige. It's been one hell of a day.

I sleep like the dead, but only after giving Gia a doctored summary of my evolved relationship with Zeno. From the looks of it, she'd been busting at the seams to find out what had happened between us. I also told her about my talk with Dad. By the time the lights clicked off, mental and emotional exhaustion carried me straight to dreamland.

When our alarm first sounds the next morning, I feel like I'm being drawn awake from a medically induced coma. I'm disoriented, and my movements are clumsy and sluggish.

"God, I could sleep for a week," I moan to the universe, in case it's listening and cares to comply.

Gia chuckles and sits up, seemingly unencumbered by my affliction. "Do you need a quick shower to wake you up? You can jump in the bathroom first if you need to."

"Nah, you go ahead. The only thing that's going to help me is sweet caffeine." I fling the covers off me and slouch ogre-like on the edge of the bed. Once I've summoned the energy to stand, I slide on some lounge pants and plod down the stairs in search of liquid energy.

When the Keurig kicks into gear, the rich aroma alone is enough to prick at my sense and liven me up. I take my full mug to the kitchen table, surprised when Livia breezes into the room.

"Morning, Isa," she says cheerily.

"You're up early. You have somewhere to be today?"

"No," she says innocently while rummaging through the fridge. "Not really."

*Okaaaay.* My spidey senses tell me something is up, but it's awfully early for her games. I sip my coffee instead and focus on waking up.

"Don't we have any orange juice in here?"

"Juice? You always have coffee in the morning."

Liv turns to grin at me and places a hand over her flat abdomen. "I don't think I'm supposed to have coffee now."

"Oh, yeah. Mom said you weren't feeling great last night."

She sucks her lips between her teeth, fighting a grin. "That's not what I meant. I'm pretty sure you aren't supposed to have caffeine … when you're pregnant."

For the briefest moment, I convince myself that I've had a stroke. It explains my exaggerated weariness and Livia's outlandish admission—I'm clearly suffering from brain damage and delusions.

It has to be.

I dazedly sip from my mug, burn my tongue, then startle enough to slosh hot coffee onto my fingers. "Goddammit!" I set down the mug and shake my hand to ease the sting.

Livia giggles and offers me a paper towel. I look between her and the coffee, a horrible surety settling in that this is real. My tongue really is burned, and Livia really did just tell me she's pregnant. I've never been so disappointed in my own good health.

"Please, tell me you're joking," I breathe.

Annoyance flashes behind her eyes. "Well, that's *rude*," she mutters. "I wasn't certain until this morning, but I took a test, and it's positive!" She stretches her arms wide and beams like the happiest woman in the world.

"Liv, you don't even have a boyfriend. How can you be so happy? Who is the father?"

"It's Nevio, of course." Her grin is eerily calculating. "I told you everything would be fine. That I'd marry someone rich and wouldn't have to scrub toilets all my life."

I'm going to be sick.

This can't be happening. If Liv is pregnant with Nevio's child, that would mean they've been having sex since … practically since he came home for the funeral. I think back to her disappearing from the lunch that day and recall all the times since that she wasn't around. When she said she'd gone out with Nevio, it never occurred to me she'd been hanging out with him for weeks already. It certainly never registered that they might have already been having sex.

Holy shit. She has no idea she's pregnant with her half brother's child.

I place my hand over my mouth to keep back the bile as Mom joins us in the kitchen.

"You look awfully pale, Isa," Mom says. "Did you get a touch of Livy's stomach bug?"

"That would be tough to do, considering it's not a stomach bug," Liv says proudly. She waits dramatically for Mom to give her full attention. "I'm pregnant, Mama.

Nevio and I are going to have a baby." My sister grins exultantly.

Mom's jaw drops, and for a second, I wonder if she knows the implications. Then she's jumping up and down and crushing Livia in a congratulatory hug. She has no idea.

So many fucking secrets, and now look where we are.

Anger and adrenaline buzz through my veins. I have to do something. I have to tell *someone*.

I could call Zeno. He definitely needs to know, but this has snowballed beyond the point of return. This isn't just about protecting his family's honor anymore—this is beyond catastrophic—and it's past time for my father to know the truth. If that angers Z, then I'll deal with him later.

"Where's Dad?" I blurt harshly, dousing their reverie.

Mom and Livia look at me quizzically.

"Why?" Mom asks. "What's gotten into you?"

"*Just tell me where the fuck Dad is!*" I scream, slapping my hand on the table.

I've completely lost my mind, and I don't have a single fuck to give.

My sister is pregnant with our brother's child.

There is only so much a person can take, and I have pushed well beyond that limit.

# CHAPTER 8

Mom's eyes bulge at my outburst. "He was meeting the gardener this morning. He left a half hour ago."

I run upstairs, grab my phone, and slide on my tennis shoes. I don't mess with socks or take time to put on my bra. Instead, I bolt down the stairs and out the back door, completely ignoring Mom's and Livia's gaping stares. The morning dew permeates my thin lounge pants as I jog through the knee-high grass on my way to Hardwick. There's a narrow path worn into the dirt where we always walk, but the tall blades of grass still arc over to graze across my shins.

Once I'm on the open lawn where the grass becomes manicured and free of trees, I run for the front of the house. Dad is talking to a younger man near one of the many flower beds. His face hardens the second he sees me running over, and he quickly ends his conversation, striding toward me to close the distance between us.

"What's wrong? Are you okay?"

I glance at the gardener, my chest heaving with exertion. The man is out of earshot, but to be safe, I lean close and speak as softly as my screaming lungs will allow. "I didn't want to tell you that I knew because Zeno asked me not to tell anyone, but Livia just announced that she's pregnant, Daddy, and I don't know what to do." As soon as the words tumble out, I know they don't make sense.

Dad's brow furrows, his eyes growing impossibly squinty. "You're going to have to slow down and explain. I'm not following you. Livy's ... pregnant?"

I take a deep breath and try to calm myself. "I know that you and Elena had an affair and that Nevio is your son. I found out that day last week when I went home sick. I wasn't so much sick as upset—not at you," I hurry to explain. "Just about everything. I said some awful things to Zeno, but we're mending that. It's beside the point. The point is, Livia announced that she's pregnant *with Nevio's baby*. Daddy, what do we do? She has no idea he's her *brother*."

Dad's eyes drift sadly toward the stone fortress that is Hardwick. "That boy always was too clever for his own good," he muses quietly before turning back to me. "I'm sorry you had to find out like this, Lulu. We've already talked about how my relationship with your mother hasn't been all that great. Not long after Gia was born, I started spending time with Elena. She was so lonely. Their relationship was primarily entered into for strategic reasons—

a sort of marriage of convenience. He needed a wife and family, but the two were never truly in love. His devotion was always to the organization. He'd spend weeks at a time in the city, and poor Elena was so young and lost. We connected in a way I've never experienced with anyone else."

His voice is tender when he speaks of her, and I wonder if he's still in love with her. Could that adoration for her be the reason he's never left Hardwick? I try to be patient as I listen. The information is fascinating, but it doesn't change the catastrophe we're facing.

"I have no good excuse for what happened next. There was a brief time when I was torn between two houses. When I learned that I was expecting children from two women at the same time, I was so ashamed. After that, I tried to keep my relationship with Elena platonic, though I wasn't perfect by any means. The one thing I did right was going to the doctor before you were even born to get a vasectomy. I didn't know where life would take me, but one thing was for certain, I wasn't having any more children. I went back to the doctor three times to make sure it wasn't a possibility. For a time, Elena made a push to strengthen her relationship with Silvano, so I did the same with your mother. When she became pregnant with Livy, though, I knew that I wasn't the only one who had strayed. I never told her that I knew. Who was I to judge her? And besides, there was no point confronting her. Elena would never divorce Silvano, and I didn't ever want to leave Elena. If your mother and I separated, she likely would have had to find another place to live, taking you girls with her. That wasn't an option. And as a single man, spending time with Elena would be inappropriate. The way things evolved sounds messy, but it worked. At least, I thought it did. I'm starting to realize how wrong I've been." He peers at me warily as if waiting for me to condemn him.

I'm dumbfounded.

Nothing in my life was what it seemed. I would think at some point I'd stop being surprised, but each new revelation blindsides me.

"So, Liv and Marca aren't yours? Who's their biological father?" I know it's not particularly relevant, but my brain is struggling to keep up.

Dad shrugs. "Don't know and don't really care. I've always considered them mine, though I'm embarrassed to say I never felt quite as invested in them as I did you and Gia. I love them. I do. But my bond with them isn't the same."

"So, that's why you weren't worried about Liv dating Nevio?"

"Exactly. While the situation isn't ideal, it's not as bad as you were thinking. Not like when you set your sights on Nevio. That was a problem on so many levels."

They aren't related. Livia may be pregnant, but she's not in an incestual relationship.

*Oh, thank God!*

I reach forward and wrap my arms around Dad's middle. "It's okay. Everything's going to be okay," I murmur, mostly for my own benefit.

Dad chuckles. "Yeah, baby girl. Everything's going to be just fine."

"Okay." I nod and pull back. "I need to talk to Zeno, though. He needs to know what's going on."

"So, he knows about me and his mom?"

"Yeah, he's known since we were kids. He saw you guys. That's why we stopped being friends, but he only explained himself recently. He was pretty upset with you for a while." I say the last part gently because I know my dad will feel awful.

He frowns and has trouble meeting my eyes. "I can't say enough how sorry I am."

"It's in the past, Daddy. I promise. Though, I need you to pretend you don't know that Zeno knows. I wasn't supposed to tell anyone, but the whole Livy thing freaked me out." Zeno's secret is escaping like water through my fingers. I can't say for certain if Dad will tell Elena. I just don't know, but the more people I tell, the higher the chances. I don't want to break Z's trust, but I felt I had no choice. The possibility of upsetting him pulls at my already frayed nerves.

"You have nothing to worry about. I won't say a thing. Now, you better go home and get dressed. Don't think you want to show up for work in wet pajamas." For once, I know the sadness in his eyes is genuine, and it makes my heart hurt. He never wanted to hurt anyone. And how could I possibly begrudge him pursuing the woman he loves. I can't, and I don't want him to feel down on himself, so I smile and keep things light.

"You're absolutely right. Thanks, Dad. I know none of this is easy, but we'll figure it out."

I wave and head back toward the cottage. As I walk, I give Zeno a call on my phone.

"Hey there." His masculine purr sends a zing straight from my ear down to my belly.

"Hey. I hope I didn't wake you." I can imagine he had a late night since he didn't leave for the city until after dark.

"Not at all. I'm actually headed to the house."

"Oh, good. We need to talk." The line is dead silent for long seconds, and I realize how that sounds. "Nothing bad, not exactly. I just need to tell you some stuff that's happened."

"I'm not sure I'm any less worried."

I huff out a laugh. "Sorry about that. Try not to stress, and I'll come find you once I'm back at the house."

"Back? Have you already been to Hardwick this morning?"

"It's a long story. I'll tell you everything when I see you."

"How could it be a long story? We haven't been apart for twelve hours yet."

Again, he has me laughing. "Things happen fast around here. Try to keep up."

He grunts and hangs up. I walk back home with renewed hope that the world isn't ending—at least, not today.

"Jesus Christ. She's fucking *pregnant*?" Zeno paces in front of the windows in his office while I sit on the sofa. I've just finished detailing everything I learned from my father and am surprised to find Z is more upset than I expected him to be.

"At least they aren't related. That would have been a disaster. And I know you didn't want my dad to know that you knew about the affair, but under the circumstances, I had to talk to him. I hope you're not upset." After thinking things through, I decided I had to admit to Z that I'd told my dad. There was no other way for me to explain knowing that Livia wasn't Dad's biological child. Besides, it's time for the secrets to come to an end. I feel better knowing I've been honest.

"I don't care about what your father knows, but I'm going to wring Nevio's fucking neck. How many *fucking* times do we have to go through this?"

His venomous words crawl along my skin like angry ants. How many times has Nevio gotten someone pregnant? This has happened before? Does Nevio have other children out there in the world?

"Z, what's going on?" I dread hearing his explanation, but I have to know the truth.

He stops and looks at me with trepidation—a worrisome emotion to see on a man like Zeno.

"My brother ... *our* brother ... is a sex addict. I didn't tell you about his issues because regardless of what you and others may think, I don't want to hurt Nevio. People with gambling or alcohol addictions aren't looked at the same as someone whose weakness is sex. At least as a man, he isn't condemned like he would be if he were a woman with the same problem. That is his only saving grace. He cheats and manipulates everyone in his life, and I know that's the addiction poisoning him, but it's hard to separate the two. He's been in and out of rehab. He has a counselor and resources, but celibacy rarely lasts long, and once he has sex, the cycle starts all over again. Sex in moderation has been beyond his reach."

I slowly list backward against the back couch cushions as I try to grasp what Zeno is telling me. I've always known Nevio was a playboy, but that's a far cry from sex addiction. When did it develop? Why? Can that type of addiction evolve out of nowhere, or did something tragic happen to trigger his disfunction?

No matter the cause, I'm devastated to hear that Nevio's issues are even worse than I'd thought. "Z, I feel terrible for him. How did this happen?"

Zeno joins me on the sofa, leaving enough space that we can face one another. "If you'll recall, I told you that we found reason to send him away after his sophomore year of school. The truth is, he had an inappropriate relationship with a teacher. According to the law, he was too young to consent, but he swore he was the one who seduced her. You know how he is—how he's always been. I don't doubt he could have been very persuasive, and the girl was in her second year of teaching, hardly older than him. It was an incredibly challenging time. My parents decided to remove him from the situation and get him counseling. While he was away, he proceeded to have sex with every female he could get close to. I'm not sure if the addiction came first or if the first relationship created the addiction. I'm not sure if he even knows. Regardless, his struggle has been a pervasive problem in his life. One he can't seem to escape."

Z pauses, his gaze distant. "The one thing he didn't allow his addiction to stain was his love for you. I think the reason he never tried to get you back in his life after school is because he wanted to protect you. He adored you—we both did—but he knew he'd only hurt you. As he suspected, once you two were together here at the estate, the craving was too much. He had to try to get with you."

Surely, the universe can only dole out so much heartbreak to one person. Have I not reached my quota? Isn't it time to sprinkle the gloom and doom on some other unsuspecting sap? I want to be angry with Nevio, but how can I be when he's clearly so broken? Instead, I'm left with an abundance of sorrow.

"He made it sound like you guys ganged up against him and sent him away out of spite."

"Sometimes, he's more honest with himself than others. When his issues are at their worst, he blames us exclusively. When he's doing better, he accepts responsibility. But I wouldn't expect him to ever reveal his darkest secrets to you voluntarily. The shame would be immeasurable."

What a horrible way to live. Every relationship is shallow at best, if not toxic and manipulative. And now, Livia has bound herself to him for life.

I close my eyes and take a deep breath. "How many children does he have out there?"

"Not as many as I might expect. There are two that I know of, and now two more are on the way. I do my best to keep apprised of his ... activities. Before Livia, he got the housekeeper, Anna, pregnant on a visit home. I'm embarrassed to admit, but he tried to coerce her into aborting the baby. When she disappeared, I worried it had something to do with him. I confronted him, and he admitted what had happened. I tracked her down as quickly as I could. I needed her to know that he didn't speak for the family and that her child was safe and would be provided for."

His explanation aligns perfectly with what Gia witnessed in the city. Poor Anna. She had to have been terrified if she thought the Mafia wanted her unborn baby dead.

Z scoots closer on the couch and angles my face with gentle fingers to get a look at my eye. "It's looking better. How does it feel?"

"Fine. It doesn't hurt too bad unless I press on the bruising." I glance down at his hand and notice for the first time that his knuckles are mottled with dried blood. My fingers drift to his wounds and ghost over the broken skin. "What happened, Z? Did you fight with someone?" I stare deep into his kaleidoscopic eyes and search for the truth, but he is an expert at concealment.

"I did what I said I'd do—I took care of things."

Aldo. That's why his knuckles are bloody.

A flutter stirs in my chest from a surge of adrenaline. "What does that mean? You can't just kill him if he worked for the family, right? I don't want him coming after me, but I don't want you to get in trouble either—with the family or the law." My heart skips into a run, pitter-pattering against the confines of my chest.

Zeno brings our foreheads together, his hands cupping my face as he seems fond of doing. I'm pretty fond of it as well. His intoxicating scent fills my lungs when we're this close. It's delicious and distracting and is zero help in calming my frantic heartbeat.

"It means he's not an issue. You'll have to leave it at that. He won't bother you again, and Grace's debt has been cleared. Forget the name Aldo Consoli ever existed."

And that's how I know Zeno De Rossi killed a man for me.

He didn't admit to it, but he doesn't have to. I know in my bones he would never allow such a threat to exist in the world. Does it bother me to know he's capable of murder?

I picture Aldo's beady eyes and shiver at the thought of his lecherous hands reaching for me. He was a disgusting excuse for a man, and I have no reservations about his death. In fact, I'm touched that Z would risk his own life and freedom to protect me in that way.

The answer is no. I'm not at all bothered by what he's done.

"Thank you, Z." I can only whisper because another set of words—three very special words—has wedged its way in my throat, but I'm not ready to release them. Not yet.

Instead, I bring my lips to his. It's meant to be a tender kiss of gratitude and affection, but it quickly morphs into something heated and carnal. He pulls me onto his lap, hands kneading firmly into my backside. Breathless, mindless minutes go by until Zeno draws his lips from mine and allows us both to settle our racing hearts.

"I'm taking you to dinner tonight."

"You are?" I smirk.

"Yeah."

"Is that your way of asking me on a date?"

"You can call it whatever you like, as long as you're there beside me."

My answering grin is effervescent. "When you put it like that, how can a girl say no?"

A satisfied rumble fills his chest while my mind drifts back to my sister.

"What are we going to do about Livy? She's convinced Nevio is going to marry her." I don't want to force them together, but I also don't want her abandoned and alone.

He releases years of frustration in a weary breath. "That is a far more complicated matter."

# CHAPTER 9

After work, I take a minute to call Grace and tell her the good news. Her debt has been forgiven.

"So, you and Zeno are together now, and he paid off my loan as like … a gift?" Her tone is incredulous. I don't blame her. It's a fantastical turn of events, and while only partly true, the result is the same.

"I know it sounds crazy, but I've was wrong about Z. We've had a lot of misunderstandings between us and have been sorting through it all. When I told him how worried I was about you, he insisted on repaying the loan. He said it was the least he could do since I'd already paid my family's debt on my own when he could have helped." I can't exactly tell her Z killed Aldo for attacking me, but I figure this makes decent sense instead.

"That is so crazy generous of him." Grace's voice wobbles with the onset of tears. "Please make sure to tell him how grateful I am. I just don't know what to say. I'm stunned. After all those years of trash-talking him … and now … you're together?"

"Well, I don't know exactly what our status is. We're having dinner tonight, so hopefully, we'll have time to talk then. It's all come about so quickly."

"No kidding! I'm hardly gone a week, and chaos erupts. I heard the Bishops are back, too. Mom was so relieved."

"So was Gia. I think she's in love with Carter, and I desperately hope this will be their shot. He seemed very attentive when we were over last night for dinner."

"They'd be perfect for each other," she says wistfully.

"What about you and Ari? Any updates there?"

"She came over, and we had an awesome day together. We've been texting a bunch. She seems so amazing. It scares me a little."

"Why would that scare you?"

"You know what they say about if something seems too good to be true."

"That's not always the case. Just take it slow and keep an open mind." It's advice I should take from myself. "Hey, Gracie, it's been good catching up, but I better get going. I need to get ready for my dinner with Z."

"I know, I know. I'll let you go, but real quick, how would that even work? Would your parents stay on as your employees if you marry him?"

"Holy crap, Grace! Slow down! We haven't even gone on a single date yet."

"Yeah, but you guys have history. It's not like you'd need a lot of time to get to know one another. I'm just saying... there is a lot to think about." She's not wrong, but I've got too many other things on my mind to worry about that now.

"*Bye*, Grace," I say playfully. "Talk to you soon."

"Always."

I end the call with a huge grin. There may be a ton of chaos going on in my life, but it's good to know my drama ended up helping my best friend. She's so upbeat on the phone that she hardly sounds like the same person.

An hour later, Zeno arrives at the house to pick me up. Something eerily similar to love stirs in my chest when he goes out of his way to shake hands with my father. It hasn't been easy for Z to push past his childhood trauma, and I appreciate that he's willing to befriend my father—someone who hurt him, even if the injury was unintentional.

We make our escape from the house with minimal fanfare. As Z reaches to open the passenger door of his car for me, he pauses with our faces inches apart. "You take my breath away, Luisa Banetti."

I'm not wearing anything too crazy—a flowy blouse over a black cotton skirt. It's dinner on a Monday night, after all. But one look from Z makes me feel like the most beautiful woman on the planet. That's the difference between him and his brother. Even before I knew about Nevio's addiction, flattery from him always felt discounted because of its abundance. When someone doles out compliments and attention like candy, it's hard to tell what's genuine and what's simply a habit. With Z, he only ever speaks with honesty when he does deign to comment on a subject.

"Glad I can return the favor," I breathe, my eyes drifting to his lips.

"*Fuck*," he groans before his mouth descends on mine.

His body presses me against the car, teasing my nipples with the warmth of his chest. The kiss is passionate but brief. When he pulls away, I can feel the effort of his restraint.

"I told myself I wouldn't devour you until after dinner … or at least the first course."

My smile has a life of its own. "If there's anyone who has mastered the art of self-restraint, it's you."

"I've never been challenged like this." He reaches for the door handle behind me and maneuvers me to the side to open the door.

"I have faith in you," I say coyly before easing into the passenger seat. I catch Zeno's responding grunt before the door clicks shut and quietly giggle to myself as he walks around to the driver's side.

Our ride to the restaurant is surprisingly pleasant. I'm not as nervous as I expected, and our conversation flows easily. It doesn't take us long to arrive at our destination, but when we do, the parking lot to the small Italian restaurant is nearly empty.

"Are you sure it's open?" I try to peer inside the heavily tinted windows, but it appears the curtains are drawn.

"I'm sure." He turns off the engine and comes around to

help me from the car. "I wanted us to have the place to ourselves."

My steps falter. "Wait. What do you mean? You reserved the whole restaurant?" I gape at him.

A small salacious smirk lifts his mouth at one corner. "I own the place, so it wasn't all that hard to do." He takes my hand, and his eyes grow serious. "I missed out on a lot of years with you. I want you to be my sole focus. No distractions."

I'm speechless. I follow his lead in a daze, wondering how I ended up in this dream-like scenario. I try to take in the restaurant's romantic atmosphere and listen to the man who directs us to a table in the center of the room, but I can't stop replaying Zeno's words in my head. It's hard to believe this is real when before, it had only existed in a secret corner of my imagination.

"You're quiet tonight," Zeno notes after we've given our drink orders and are alone again.

I sip from my water glass, giving me a moment to put together the right words. "It's a little hard to wrap my head around how different things suddenly are. You were so … cold toward me for so long, and now you're thoughtful and attentive. It's a lot to process."

"I've always been attentive where you're concerned. You simply never knew it."

Our server brings over the bottle of wine Z selected and pours us each a glass before disappearing.

"You have to explain." I shake my head. "No more secrets or vague innuendoes. Not if I'm going to trust you."

He dips his chin in acquiescence. "Once you moved to

the city, and I matured enough to accept that you were innocent in your father's actions, I started to keep eyes on you. I've always felt it was my job to protect you, even if at a distance."

"You had people *watching* me?"

"You weren't being followed or anything—nothing so... invasive. I made sure to look into your roommates ... or ... *other* people who came into your life. Employers. Professors. Boyfriends. Nothing crazy. I simply made sure the people around you weren't a threat."

"I think you and I have a different definition of crazy." I gape at him, shaking my head. "That's not exactly normal, Zeno."

His voice reverberates deep from his chest. "Who says I'm normal?"

*He's right. Nothing about this man is average.*

He lifts his wineglass to take a sip, and I'm transfixed by the dichotomy of the delicate glass gently propped between his masculine fingers. I have to force myself to focus on our conversation.

"It would seem you know all about my years in the city, but I don't know much about your life at all."

"What would you like to know?"

*Everything.*

I shrug. "I spoke with Savio the morning after we all had dinner."

"Did you?"

I detect the tiniest stiffening of his spine and wonder if it's curiosity or a touch of jealousy.

"I did. He told me how you two started working for the family at the same time and indicated you became close."

"We are. He's one of the few people I'd consider a true friend."

"It's a shame Christiano has pitted you two against one another."

"That's his way. He wants his family at the helm, but Savio has no desire to be the face of the organization. He and I decided years ago that I would make a push for boss, and he would be my consigliere."

This is the first I'm hearing directly from Z about his ambitions, and the fact that he's willing to share something so private thrills me, though the rush is tampered with reservation. I knew he was aiming to take over his father's role as underboss, but becoming boss of a Mafia family is a whole other level of responsibility. Of visibility.

"Do you think that'll happen?" I ask, sipping my wine.

"It's hard to say what will happen. Christiano wants Savio to succeed him. He's hell-bent on having his blood in leadership. And Savio is under immense pressure to give his uncle what he wants."

"That's so ridiculous. You'd be a better leader, and if you want the job, giving it to someone else because of their genes is absurd." I'm surprised I'm so defensive on Zeno's behalf. I don't even necessarily want him to be the boss, but I don't want someone stealing away the position if it's something he truly desires.

The corners of his lips quirk upward. "You always did call things like you saw them."

"Yeah, but how I saw it wasn't always right." My eyes

trace the tines of the fork at my place setting, unwilling to meet Zeno's gaze when I think of the horrible things I've said to him. "I've been pretty embarrassed about how wrong I've been."

"The only person in this room who should feel any remorse is me. You handled a difficult situation with strength, dignity, and as much empathy as humanly possible. I don't deserve you, Isa, but I'll take every part of you I can get."

Our gazes lock in such a heated, intimate exchange that I'm almost relieved when the server arrives to take our orders. I'm terrified of how quickly my heart is reshaping itself to make room for Z. It's almost as if an echo of him kept his presence alive and allowed him to take up residence as though he were never gone. The seamless transition wouldn't have been possible if my heart hadn't clung to the hope of his return. I hadn't realized it was the case, but I'd never fully given up on our story.

We spend over an hour talking about everything under the sun. Nothing too heavy. Just two old friends getting to know one another again. The food is exceptional, and the candlelit setting enables us to get lost in our own private oasis where none of the drama of reality can touch us. Time slips by without awareness until my bladder insists I step away to the restroom. When I return, the table has been cleared, and Z is leaning back in his chair with a storm brewing in his eyes.

"Everything okay?" I slow as I approach the table. The melodic strains of an acoustic guitar drift in the air around us, filling the empty room with anticipation.

Zeno stands and stalks around the table to me before I have a chance to sit. "I told myself not to push you—to let you come to me on your own and that you being here was enough—but I want more. I want to hear you say that you're mine."

Maybe it's the wine.

Maybe it's just Z, but I have no reservations about giving him what he wants because it's what I want too.

"I could never be anyone else's," I admit in a quiet but steady voice.

In one swift motion, he scoops me up and sets me on the table. His body presses close, spreading my legs to make room for him and easing my skirt up my thighs. My lips part on a gasp, and Z uses the opportunity to possess me, slanting his lips over mine with ravenous hunger. Fisting a hand in my hair, he tugs my head back to expose my neck. He lays siege to the delicate skin, teeth grazing and tongue laving a path down to my chest. When his knees drop to the floor, eyes burning my face as they drink me in, I realize his plan to devour me was no exaggeration.

"Z, we can't. Someone will see." My breathless objection lacks conviction.

"I sent the others home. It's just you—" His nose grazes my slit through the silk of my thong. "And me." His lips close over my core, coaxing a dizzying rush of blood to my clit.

"No one?" I ask dazedly.

"No one. I don't share what's mine."

My knees spread, spurred by my need for more. I'm about to tell Z to take off my panties when I hear the rip of fabric and feel the warm caress of his breath on my bare center. I moan with anticipation, leaning back on my hands as my eyes roll up to the ceiling. I'm rewarded with languorous licks from his rough tongue. Long, seductive touches that light my body on fire.

"*Yes*, Zeno. That feels so good."

I realize my eyes have drifted shut when cool air signals the loss of Z's delectable mouth. I crack my lids open to see him take a long swig of water. He watches me with predatory awareness. A hunter's warning that he'd be on me if I made the slightest move. So I sit still and wait. Pleasure coiling. Madness looms, and my inner muscles clench with frenzied need as Zeno rolls an ice cube around his mouth.

When his tongue returns to my slit, a burst of cold blasts me with a hunger so intense it clamps down on my lungs. The icy sensation causes a fever to spark through my veins, heating my core and electrifying my nerve endings. An overwhelming, chaotic energy quickly builds between my legs and deep into my belly. It swells and teases, but before it can reach its pinnacle, Zeno pulls away.

He rises to his feet and begins to undo his belt. "Turn around." His coarse, animalistic command licks down my spine. It doesn't just slide over my skin—the demand sinks down into the marrow of my bones, floods my bloodstream, and overwhelms my senses.

I am completely entranced.

Mesmerized and drunk off my need for the enigmatic man before me.

Without hesitation, I slide from the table and turn as I was instructed. Zeno's hands are instantly on my hips, lifting my skirt to fully expose me from the waist down. The heat from his body blankets my back. One hand snakes around to cup the delicate part of my throat while the other drifts down to my core.

"Me being inside you is different from you giving yourself to me body and soul. Now that you've done that, there's no going back. Do you understand?"

Z waits for me to nod before folding us down, his body pressing my chest onto the white tablecloth. My hands brace against the table on either side of me. The searing heat of his cock settles perfectly in the crease between my cheeks, and I arch my back in invitation. He angles himself at my entrance when I realize I never heard him put on a condom.

"You didn't ask if I'm on birth control," I note absently. I'm on the pill, so I'm not worried about pregnancy, but he doesn't know that, right? Surely, his monitoring activities hadn't been that detailed.

"That's because I don't care," he murmurs against my neck, his cock gliding sensually along my slit. "I'm going to get you pregnant one of these days, and if it happens now, well, then it happens. We're not getting any younger, Isa. Plus, I'm clean, so that's not a concern."

"You don't know if I'm clean."

"Aside from trusting that you would tell me if there was something I should know, I'm going to spend the rest of my life fucking your beautiful body, so whatever you might have will be mine sooner or later. For better—" Z accents his words by slipping his throbbing cock an inch inside me. "Or worse." He thrusts again, voice straining.

I vaguely wonder at his choice of words but only for a second. The fullness inside me is too distracting to hold any thought except for a relentless need for more. He pounds into me from behind, quickly elevating to a merciless rhythm. Zeno manages to make our carnal position feel intimate and connected by keeping his body close to mine, his arms holding me like a precious treasure he can't stand to part with. When one hand lowers to reach between my thighs, I claw at the table beneath me, trying to process the sheer volume of sensation.

Breathless gasps tumble from my lips.

Pleasure commands every inch of me. Sweeps me away and traps me beneath a wave of liquid lightning. My body begins to shudder violently. Thousands of tiny fireworks ignite inside me, bursting from my core out to my fingers and toes as my inner muscles squeeze to the breaking point.

"Jesus, *fuck*," he hisses between labored breaths as his own release crashes over him. He squeezes me until I can't breathe, but I don't care. I don't need air when I'm full of Zeno.

My lungs argue differently, but lucky for them, he eases his hold as our twitching muscles calm in tandem. Our panting breaths slow enough that the gentle strains of music playing in the background return to my awareness.

When Z slides himself slowly in and out of me, his softening length still plenty solid to stir my insides, a purr sounds from deep in my throat.

"That feels so good," I murmur.

"It feels incredible. I've never been in a woman without

a condom." His admission stuns me. It would mean either he's never had a girlfriend—which I find hard to believe—or he's never trusted anyone enough to go bare. No one until me.

I twist to meet his eyes. "Are you serious?"

Z lifts off me, helping me up. "I am." He takes a cloth napkin draped over the back of his chair and uses it to wipe the arousal from between my legs. "I watched the destruction that resulted from infidelity, and I wasn't willing to chance permanent ties to someone I wasn't certain about."

"What makes you certain about me?" I ask in a whisper.

He presses his cheek to mine, breathing in my post-orgasmic flush. "You're my Isa. I've never been more certain about anything in my life." He brings our lips together in a kiss that is tender yet passionate and totally intoxicating.

Zeno stuffs the napkin in his back pocket and helps right my clothing.

"Will you come back to Hardwick with me?" he asks after helping me into the car.

His invitation is incredibly tempting. I want to join him, but I also don't want to rush things. To risk losing the incredible feeling I get whenever I'm around him.

"I think I should probably head home. I have to work tomorrow, and there's the whole thing about you being my boss…"

"Is that really going to keep you from sleeping in my bed?"

I shrug. "It's not just that. Our families have a lot of

history—*we* have a lot of history—and I don't want to screw things up by rushing."

"I can respect that, but your idea of rushing may be different than mine." He closes the door, a wolfish grin teasing his lips as he disappears from view.

# CHAPTER 10

"You're up early again." I find Livia wrapped in a blanket at the kitchen table when I come down the next morning.

"I had to pee, and then my stomach didn't feel so great. Figured I'd try to eat some crackers, but once I got down here, I decided I couldn't eat anything." All her bubbling enthusiasm from the day before is gone. It could be the sickness or her winning morning personality, but I wonder if there's more to it.

"Have you told Nevio the news?"

"Yeah. He was supposed to come out here last night, but something came up." She's so incredibly naïve that my heart hurts for her.

I sit down in the chair next to her. "Livy, honey. You might want to consider the possibility that Nevio could struggle with the news of an unplanned pregnancy. That's a lot for a person to take in." I use my best Gia voice and choose my words with the utmost care. My goal isn't to hurt her, despite her clear and obvious reaction otherwise.

Spine rigid, she glares at me. "You don't know anything. He just doesn't want to come out here because you're so hateful to him. He's *thrilled* about the baby, and I have no doubt we'll be married in no time." She gathers her blanket and leaves the table, storming back upstairs.

*That went about as well as could be expected.*

Daddy always said you can lead a horse to water, but you can't force it to drink. Livia will always be that horse. She will never learn from others' mistakes or take advice she doesn't want to hear. It's unfortunate, but it's not my problem.

I heave out a sigh and continue with my morning routine. My evening with Zeno was too good for Livia to spoil my bright new outlook.

Once I'm at Hardwick, Elena stops by the kitchen to ask for a word with me. I'm curious but not overly concerned. She doesn't seem upset, and I can't think of a reason for me to be in trouble. I can't imagine she'd have a problem with Zeno and me being together, though stranger things have happened. Lately, strange has become the new normal.

I follow her to the sitting area off the main entry and take a seat in an armchair opposite her. "Is everything all right?"

"Oh, yes." She smiles warmly. "Zeno told me that you know about Nevio's struggles, and I wanted to talk to you about it myself. It hasn't been easy dealing with his issues and being unable to talk to anyone about it for fear of hurting him just adds another degree of difficulty."

"I can't even imagine."

"When we first sent him to boarding school, I cried for days. Silvano assured me that Nevio would be better off in a different environment, but I was so worried. I suppose the thing that helped me cope the most was knowing that Nevio and Silvano were getting space from each other. I always wondered if their strained relationship contributed to Nevio's problems. Silvano was so hard on him. He tried to toughen up Nevio because he thought my gentle boy was too soft." Her words are tortured. What a terrible position to have been in.

I'm endlessly curious about whether Silvano knew Nevio wasn't his and if that contributed to the strain in their relationship. It wasn't Nevio's fault he was the product of an affair. Yet my own father had expressed how the same circumstances had impacted his paternal feelings for my younger sisters. Maybe Silvano had faced a similar challenge.

Poor Nevio. It's no wonder he's a mess.

"There's never any way to know if what we're doing is best. You've always loved Nevio with your whole heart and done everything you can for him. That's all any child can ask of a parent." I try to give her the only assurance I can.

"We both did. Silvano's parenting may have seemed harsh, but he was trying to prepare Nevio for the realities of our world. As you know, we live with dangers other people only experience in the movies."

"Unfortunately, yes. I do know."

Elena nods and takes hold of my hand. "I'm glad Z told you all this. It'll make things easier in the days ahead. He told me about Livia and the baby. I've always wondered if our families might be connected one day, but that wasn't quite what I'd envisioned." Her blue eyes fill with worry. For once, she almost looks her age.

"You never know what the future holds." I smile and squeeze her hand as the doorbell chimes in the entry.

"I wonder who that could be." Elena stands, and I follow suit with plans to return to the kitchen, but when we reach the front door, Zeno is there greeting Christiano De Bellis.

"Come in," Z greets him. "To what do we owe this pleasant surprise?"

Christiano tips his head in an exaggerated bow to Elena and me. "I didn't mean to disturb the entire household, but it's lovely to see you both."

"Always a pleasure, Christiano." Elena gives the older man a hug while I hope my smile and wave suffice as greeting enough. I don't want to come off as rude, but I really don't want to hug him.

"Would you like to come have a seat?" Elena motions toward the sitting area. "I'm happy to get you a drink as well."

"Oh, no. I only stopped by for a moment to invite you all to dinner tonight. Ari will be at the house, and I know how much she enjoys seeing you, Z." He turns his calculating gaze from Zeno to me. His attention crawls across my skin like an army of angry spiders. "And the invitation includes you, Miss Banetti, if you don't already have plans."

I am a deer in headlights. Am I supposed to accept or politely decline?

"Of course, I'd love to come," I stutter my response, quickly defaulting to acceptance where the boss is concerned. He's not the type to extend an invitation if he doesn't want someone present, though I have no clue why he'd want me to join them. Dinner at the De Bellis house is the absolute *last* thing I wanted to do tonight.

"Perfect," he croons.

The little hairs on the back of my neck stand at attention. Something about Christiano gives me the creeps. It's hard to know the exact source when there are so many options to choose from. But it's there in the way he looks at people and his tone of speech. Condescension. Manipulation.

Being in his presence leaves me coated in an oily residue that not even a good scrubbing can cleanse away. And now I have to spend my evening clogging my pores with his filth.

I shiver from top to bottom the second the front door closes behind him.

CHRISTIANO'S TUXEDO PARK home is on the opposite side of the lake and around a bend so that it can't be seen from the De Rossi property. It's traditional compared to his city apartment, but the home isn't a historic masterpiece like Hardwick. Situated closer to the water, Christiano's house is a Spanish-style mansion set upon retaining walls constructed of large river rocks. The home stands out from the landscape, unlike other properties tucked away in the trees. It's not surprising. Christiano doesn't do subtle.

He welcomes us with freshly poured champagne, then offers to give a tour of the estate. His motivation must be his own ego because I know he doesn't care about my opinion of him, and the De Rossis are doubtless already familiar with the home. It's an opportunity to tout his own affluence. It is unnecessary, but I appreciate the show, nonetheless, because it kills time and gives further insight into the man who runs the Giordano family.

I lean in and speak softly to Z as we trail behind Christiano and Elena. "It strikes me as somewhat odd that you guys choose to live out here. Seems like it would be more convenient to live in the city."

"Years ago, the Five Families all went underground in the nineties to escape federal scrutiny—not only our enterprises but also our physical presence. You can't have a target on your back if you're invisible. When the internet enabled the existence of online business, there was even less reason to stay in the city. You won't find made men sitting around tables in Little Italy anymore. Times have changed."

"Your dad spent an awful lot of time in the city. Do you think you'd have to do the same?" I wouldn't want to be left behind like Elena. I'm not sure what went on between her and Silvano, but I would prefer not to live in a separate city than my husband. I'm getting ahead of myself, but it's a topic that needs to be brought up eventually if Zeno and I are considering a life together.

"Time in the city isn't always necessary. I know for my dad, it was a matter of dedication to the family and his work. He was hands-on and wanted to be present rather than rely on a representative to report back to him." His words are infused with respect for his father.

Silvano's choices don't resonate with me the same as they do with Zeno, but I don't want to speak poorly of the dead. Z's father put work above his wife and children. Mafia men may feel like their organization constitutes more than a simple employer, but the truth is, once these men die, they are replaced and forgotten as quickly as any other employee. But Elena and Zeno and Nevio—they'll hold tight to Silvano's memory. They'll love and honor him long after he's gone, which is why they deserved his time while he was alive, not some capitalist organization. I doubt Z would see things in the same light.

When we make our way back to the main living area, Ari is there sipping from a crystal glass.

"Ah, there's my Arianna," Christiano calls with a plastic grin. "I'm sure Zeno has been anxious to see you. Come join us."

Z stiffens then crosses to kiss Ari on each cheek. "You look lovely, as always."

She gives him a thin smile before her eyes flit to mine. Pink ghosts the smooth skin on the tops of her cheekbones. "Hey, Z. Luisa, Elena, it's great to see you both."

I can't discern what's going on. Is it embarrassment coloring her otherwise flawless complexion? What does she have to be embarrassed about? I'm the obvious fifth wheel in the group.

"Will Savio be joining us this evening?" Zeno asks our host.

"No, I knew you'd want time with Ari, so I decided we'd keep things more intimate. You two should be spending as much time together as possible." He raises his brows and grins, cutting a sly glance in my direction as he turns. "I believe dinner is ready if we'd like to move to the dining room."

Why the over-the-top innuendo about Z and Ari? Does Christiano know that Zeno and I have started seeing one another? What other reason is there for his behavior? I'd swear he's trying to send me a message that Zeno is spoken for, and I shouldn't waste my time. But Z and Ari don't want to marry one another. His intentional ignorance of their interests elsewhere is unsettling. I can't be the only one suffocating in the awkwardness.

When I look at Z, my eyes round with disbelief. He appears totally unaffected. Impassive and even a touch bored. Doesn't it bother him that his boss is still planning his future with another woman? He wouldn't ever agree to a loveless marriage like that, would he? Surely not after watching his parents live separate lives.

Then I recall our discussion the night before about his desire to become boss of the family one day. He and Savio have been planning their ascension for years, strategizing and biding their time. Zeno needs this promotion to underboss in order to make that dream a reality.

Is this how things unfolded for Silvano? Had he fallen in love with a woman unacceptable in the eyes of the family and married for power? Is *that* why he spent so much time in the city? Two homes with two separate lives? It would make sense.

How would Zeno look upon such an arrangement? Would the Mafia culture have molded his perspective in a way that enabled him to justify such a situation? Maybe he's come to believe it wouldn't be so terrible to have his cake and eat it too. He could marry Ari, become boss, and keep me as his dirty little secret in an apartment in the city. Maybe he considers that a normal part of Mafia life.

Is there a chance I had assumed his devotion to me meant marriage while he had assumed something totally different? We haven't been together long enough to have that kind of deep discussion, but it makes sense. It would explain why he would be affectionate with me at the Bishops' house, then cool and distant here in front of his Mafia family. He hasn't made a single move to show any attachment to me. If anything, he's kept a discerning distance between us.

My crystal champagne flute clanks on the table when I lower it distractedly.

I feel sick to my stomach.

I want to run from the house, but I absolutely must keep my composure. I could be blowing things out of proportion. We haven't even been at the house for an hour. Yet I look between Ari and Zeno, two powerful, confident individuals, and watch as they dance to Christiano's manic beat. I've yet to see either of them stand up to the man. Would they ever? What would Christiano do if they did reject his machinations?

I'm not sure I'd like the answer.

The entire train of thought sends me plummeting to a dark place. My contribution to the dinner conversation is mechanical at best. I chew my food without tasting it. I smile on cue and dance like a good marionette. Like Zeno and Ari and everyone else who surrounds Christiano De Bellis.

By the time we pull away from the table, I'm disgusted with myself. Not for playing my part at dinner because that was necessary. I'm upset that I let myself think I could have Zeno when I knew he was intended for someone else. I let his words assure me, but his actions speak differently, at least when his Mafia family is present. There's been no reassuring kisses or gentle touches. If I'd been a fly on the wall, I would never have suspected he'd been tossing around "for better or worse" twenty-four hours earlier.

When I allow our history to color events, I'm even more ashamed of myself. That I'd jump into his deep waters without the slightest thought for my safety. With his history of brushing me off, how could I have been so careless? I told him I wanted to take things slow, but I'd forgotten to tell my heart the same.

His willingness to kill for me says nothing about his intent to marry me. I don't doubt his devotion. It's his priorities that worry me. Will he place his obligations to Christiano above his feelings for me?

If his behavior tonight is any indication, then I have my answer.

Frustration and hurt threaten to overwhelm me. I need a moment alone to compose myself.

Before I take a seat in the living area where we've gathered for after-dinner drinks, I ask Ari to point me in the direction of the restrooms.

"Let me show you," she offers. "It's a little tucked away—you know these old houses." Once we're in the adjoining room, she presses a panel in the wall, which opens to reveal a well-disguised powder room. "There you go!"

"Ari, wait a sec." I hadn't planned to have a private conversation with her, but now that the opportunity has arisen, I have to seize the moment.

She turns back toward me, expression guarded.

"I want to talk to you about Grace. She's so much more sensitive than either of us. I don't know what your intentions are, and I'm not meaning to imply you're out to hurt her, but I ask that you treat her with compassion. If ... *circumstances* ... will force you to walk away from her, don't lead her on. She really likes you, and I don't want her to get hurt."

I don't want Grace to be Ari's dirty secret anymore than I want to be Zeno's.

A flash of indignation passes behind her eyes. "My life is complicated," she says stiffly.

My gaze drifts toward the living area where masculine voices carry in the air. "I'm beginning to understand that. It's why I wanted to say something." I meet her arctic stare and brace for my next question. "If it comes to it, would you marry him?" This is the question I most wanted to ask.

Her reaction is visceral. Nostrils flare. Jaw clenches.

She opens her mouth to respond, then clamps her lips shut. With a quick spin and several purposeful strides in her red-bottomed stilettos, she's left me standing alone, no closer to an answer.

I take a shaky breath and wish I could slip out a back door. Instead, I use my trip to the restroom to compose myself and march back to the battlefield.

An hour later, I'm finally granted my freedom when we climb back into the car and head for home. We are all silent on the short drive. My thoughts filter down to a single question. Would I still want to marry Zeno if I knew our marriage would deny him his lifetime ambition? I would love for him to stand up to Christiano, but I would also feel terrible if he lost everything because of me. I keep picturing my father, who chose his commitment to my mother over the family. That didn't play out so well for him. Even if Z was willing to reject Ari, would I want him to be forced to make that kind of decision?

No, I wouldn't. But it's also not my place to steal the choice from him either.

I hate my limited options, no matter how I look at them. And even more so, I hate Christiano De Bellis for imposing his will on other people's lives.

When Z pulls up at my parents' house, I open the back seat door with the last of my strength. The night's mental gymnastics have left me completely drained.

Zeno steps from the car and snags my hand. "Wait, Isa."

I slow, unable to argue.

"I'm sorry about tonight. I know that couldn't have been easy."

I slip my hand from his grasp. "Just tell me now, don't drag it out. Are you going to refuse him or not?" If Zeno and Ari are destined to marry, there's no point in pretending otherwise. A simple yes or no, and we can all move on.

"I'm going to handle it," he barks gruffly.

It's not enough. I need an answer that doesn't leave room for me to become his woman on the side. "Are. You. Going. To. Refuse. Him?"

"It's not that simple, Isa. *Christ.*" He rakes his hands through his hair in frustration.

And just like that, my heart splits wide open all over again. As much as I didn't want him to have to choose between me and his ambitions, I still wanted him to pick me. To choose me above our parents' indiscretions and his boss's ploys and all the other obstacles that have come between us.

Tears pool in my eyes. "You're wrong," I whisper, then walk calmly to the house, both relieved and brokenhearted that he makes no move to stop me.

# CHAPTER 11

Two days pass without a word from Z.

He left for the city the morning after dinner at Christiano's. I don't reach out to him because he is the only one who can fix this. I made my feelings known, and if he isn't ready to commit to me, then I won't beg him. Granted, a part of me hoped the time apart would help him see things more clearly. Help him realize how much he wants me at his side. But with each passing hour, my hope for such a result dwindles.

I can't say where his mind is at, but our time apart has revealed to me how empty my life feels without him. The realization of how attached I've become is terrifying. What if he doesn't choose me?

*Then you'll scrape yourself off the floor and keep going.*

I will, but that's not what I want. I want Z. Losing him

would hurt dearly. I would have to cut him from my life completely because anything short of calling him mine would be too painful. I've seen a glimpse of what it would feel like to be the center of his world, and I can't accept a casual friendship knowing what could have been. Either he becomes the air I breathe, or I bury a part of myself along with all thoughts of him. There is no in-between.

Livia left for the city the same day as Zeno and hasn't contacted us since, so aside from my troubles with Z, I've worried incessantly about my sister. Mom is convinced Liv and Nevio are off celebrating like blissed-out lovebirds. I wish I could buy into the fantasy, but I know better.

Would Nevio say horrible, hurtful things to her if she pushed for a commitment? How would Livy respond if he did? She's brash and emotional on a good day. I can only imagine how she'd behave with pregnancy hormones flooding her system. Would she feel desperate if he rejects her? Being a young, unwed mother is a long way to fall from landing a rich husband.

Thankfully, Gia's incandescent happiness shines brightly through my gloom and gives my spirits a touch of buoyancy. She flits around the house with boundless energy and is more talkative than I've ever seen her in all our years. In fact, she's been preoccupied enough with her own budding relationship that she hasn't been around enough to ask about mine. I appreciate the distraction because I wouldn't know what to tell her if she did ask questions.

As with the two previous evenings, the second we arrive home from work on Friday, Gia freshens up in record time before heading next door to spend her evening with Carter and the kids. I smile at her retreating form as I check the fridge for dinner options. Mom sits at the table, scrolling through her phone, and Dad has yet to come home. If I want a meal, I'll have to manage on my own.

I'm pulling sausage from the fridge when the front door swings open, and Livy's cheerful greeting carries to the back of the house.

"Hey, everyone! I'm home!" She sweeps into the kitchen and beams at Mom and me. "I've got news," she sings, flattening her palm against her chest to display an enormous diamond ring on her finger.

Mom starts screaming. "You did it, Livy! You did it!" She flings her arms around my sister, and the two begin to jump in tandem.

I'm as floored as my mother but for completely different reasons. He proposed. He actually did it. And now my sister will be married to a philandering, pathological liar. She won't want for money, but I can't imagine she'll ever truly be happy. And the craziest part is, even if I told her the truth about Nevio, I don't think it would change a thing. She'd still walk down that aisle at the end of the day, determined as ever.

So instead of crying the tears that scream to break free, instead of begging and pleading with her to see reason, I plaster on a brittle smile and congratulate my little sister.

"You must be so excited, Livy. I hope you two will be blissfully happy together." I give her a hug and say a prayer that they somehow beat the odds and find happiness. Their start will be even rockier than my parents', which hasn't ended well. But there is always hope, even if only the tiniest sliver.

Liv will get what she wants—to be taken care of—so maybe that's all she truly needs to believe she's happy. Happiness is relative, after all.

"We are over the moon," she croons. "I wish we had time for a proper wedding, though, but I don't want to look all fat in my wedding pictures, and the countdown is on." She rubs her still flat belly with her newly blinged-out hand. "We're thinking only a month or so before we tie the knot." She explains the situation with exaggerated nonchalance. Her expectation is that we'll squawk and fawn over her, and while my mother has no problem falling in line, my generosity will only go so far.

I sit back and watch as the two of them dive into wedding discussions. Rather than thinking of colors and flowers, I contemplate how Zeno managed to accomplish such a feat. The engagement had to have resulted from his influence, and Nevio isn't fond of his brother enough to be guilted into a wedding. He couldn't care less if Zeno was upset with him.

After thinking it over, I'm increasingly curious about Zeno's activities during the past few days.

We all eat dinner together, save for Gia. Dad gives Livy his congratulations, and Marca practically bounces in her seat at the prospect of her sister moving in next door. I know that will never happen, but I'm not about to say anything. As soon as we finish eating, Livia sidesteps cleanup to go show friends her new ring. I force Marca to give me a hand with cleanup, though she disappears the second her duties are completed. I wind up with the living room to myself, grateful for the rare opportunity to zone out while flipping channels until my mother's shrill voice fills my ears.

*"Is this some kind of joke?"*

My parents' bedroom is right off the living room, so when Mom comes charging out, I'm smack in the middle of their argument. I consider slipping upstairs but am too curious to move when she waves a stack of papers in the air.

"I'm not signing *anything*. You can take these back to your lawyer and ask for your money back." She shoves them into Dad's chest, forcing him to take the papers.

Dad is calm and collected, as always. He isn't letting himself get sucked into Mom's tornado of agitation. "It's your call, but not signing doesn't make them go away. It just means the sheriff will come serve you instead. I'm trying to do this in the least painful way possible. It's time, Gemma."

Papers? Served by the sheriff? Is Dad filing for *divorce*?

I'm stunned. That has to be it, but I never thought he'd go through with it. I'd hoped, but after so many years together, I figured that he'd be reluctant to take the plunge.

"I know no such thing. What about the girls? What about all the years we've been together? You think you can just walk out like we mean *nothing*?" Mom spits at him.

"You think you can go behind my back and put us into debt with the family, then have your fucking bookie show up at our home and threaten our girls? Make them pay for your mistakes?" Seething fury slithers under his skin, a warning as deadly as any rattlesnake. Dad is more upset than I realized. "Of course the past has meaning, but that doesn't change where we're at. We haven't been a couple for a long time, and you know it."

Mom gapes at him for an elongated second before stiffening her spine. "I'm not the only one who's messed up over the years," she hisses, still undeterred by his unexpected show of strength. Mom's been trampling over my father for years without consequence and is unable to understand that his patience has ended. She thinks she can use blackmail to keep him—threaten to tell his secrets if he won't stay. I get the sense she knows about Elena and Nevio and intends to use the information as leverage.

Judging by Daddy's reaction, she should have reconsidered her tactic.

My father goes eerily still. He's only six inches taller than her, but under the weight of his murderous stare, he looks like a giant. "You sure you want to go there, Gemma? Because Liv and Marca might not be happy with how that conversation ends." Ever so slowly, he drags his gaze from Mom to me, drawing her manic stare with him. Dad's not afraid to play dirty either. He's been hoarding his own secrets, and while I already know the truth, Mom doesn't know that.

I gape wide-eyed at the two of them, desperate not to be dragged into the middle but unable to give up my front-row seat to this showdown.

All the blood drains from Mom's face. If she outs Dad, he'll make sure everyone knows Liv and Marca aren't his. Using the girls against her is ugly, but I can't entirely blame him. Mom dragged them both down into the dirt—he's only following her lead.

"Give me a fucking pen," she spits, snagging the papers and a pen from Dad. She scribbles out a signature on the top page, muttering something about not knowing what she's supposed to do all on her own. "Does this mean I have to find a new job? You got me knocked up as a child, and now you're going to throw me out with no job prospects, no education, and no money? This is some *bullshit*, Tony." She tosses the papers at Dad and storms back into their room, slamming the door behind her.

She never did understand that the world didn't owe her anything. That even people who are handed money and power still have to earn respect and deserve the love of the people around them if they want genuine relationships. Mom drains the relationship bank dry then doesn't understand why her balance is zero. Even in her fifties, she still doesn't get it.

Dad lowers himself onto the couch, suddenly moving like a man decades older, sighing as he comes to rest beside me. "I'm sorry you had to witness that, Lulu."

"It's okay, Daddy. I'm proud of you for going through with it. I know it isn't easy."

"I called my lawyer the minute you told me about her debt with the bookie. That's who I went to see while I was in the city with Mom and the girls. Should have done this ages ago."

"Change is hard." I scoot in closer and lay my head on his shoulder.

Dad glances back toward their bedroom. "Doubt this'll

be pretty. She has no money for an attorney, so that might help, but she'll find ways to lash out."

"Probably, but you're a good man. I know you won't be unnecessarily harsh on her. She's still our mom."

His cheek comes to rest against my head, and I breathe in the subtle scent of cherry cigars that lingers on his clothes.

"That's the one thing I'll always be grateful for—she gave me you girls. The very best part of my world."

We sit like that for long minutes, each lost in our own thoughts. I wanted to give Zeno time to sort out his feelings, but time is up. Watching my parents' marriage crumble has made me realize the importance of communication. I want us to talk in person, so it will have to wait until tomorrow, but one way or another, we are going to hash out or differences.

Zeno is a special man. I'd be remiss if I didn't work to keep him in my life. My pride had convinced me that fighting for a relationship was groveling and beneath me, but that's not always the case. If I want Zeno to stand up to Christiano for me, I should be willing to make an effort as well—lay my fears aside and do everything in my power to give us a chance at love. He's worth it. *We* are worth it.

# CHAPTER 12

THE SMELL OF BACON FRYING ROUSES ME FROM SLEEP THE next morning. When I head downstairs to investigate, I note a pillow and several blankets on the sofa. Dad's new bed for the time being. The sight should make me sad, but more than anything, I think I'm relieved. If there's any sadness in the circumstances, it's that I'll worry less about Dad on his own than I would if he was still married to Mom. It's too bad things couldn't be different, but it is what it is. The door to the master bedroom is shut, and I can only assume Mom won't be coming out anytime soon. It's going to take some time for her to process.

In the kitchen, Dad is stationed at one skillet while Gia flips pancakes at another. Marca and Livia both sit at the table, looking at their phones.

"You guys do know it's Saturday morning, right?" I

tease. My family has never slept super late, but this is a tad unusual, even for us.

Gia grins. "Carter and I are taking the kids to the zoo today, so I had to get an early start." She'd crept in late last night, and I didn't want to keep her awake with news of Dad filing for divorce, so I didn't say anything yet. By the sound of things, the news will have to wait a little longer.

"That sounds like fun. I haven't been to the zoo in ages."

"You're welcome to join us!"

"Maybe another time, but thanks for the invite." I have more pressing matters to deal with.

Livia drops her phone on the table and shoots a look at Marca. "Well, I'd still be asleep if this one had remembered to silence her phone."

"Don't blame me!" Marca shoots back. "You're the one who tossed and turned for fifteen minutes, grumbling about your bladder."

"It wouldn't have been an issue if your phone hadn't woken me in the first place. I don't know what the deal is, but I'm already peeing all the time. This thing isn't big enough to press on my bladder. I even had to make Zeno stop on the way back from the city last night. Can you believe that? I haven't stopped at a gas station to pee on a trip from the city since I was a kid." She shakes her head and resumes scrolling.

"Zeno drove you back home?" That would mean he's at Hardwick.

"Yeah, isn't that sweet of him? I mean, we *are* going to be family soon, but still. Nevio had some things to handle, or he would have brought me back himself."

*Right. Sure he would have.*

"Who's ready for the first plate?" Gia calls out.

Marca leaps up. Livia groans.

I consider going straight over to find Z but decide it's a little early to surprise him with a heavy conversation. I'd be better off giving him a chance to wake up first, and that would allow me time to eat with my family and get cleaned up.

An hour later, I tread through the grass between our houses like I've done thousands of times before. For years, this walk brought on trepidation and anxiety, but today those emotions are balanced with an equal measure of hope. The sun reflects my optimism as it blankets the landscape in warmth.

My visit is unannounced, so I go to the front of the house and ring the bell.

Elena greets me with a grin. "Good morning, Isa. What brings you over?" She steps aside and welcomes me inside.

"I heard Zeno came back last night and was hoping to talk to him."

"He stayed the night but got up early and left. I'm afraid you've missed him."

Disappointment tugs at my shoulders. "Oh, that's too bad."

"I can try to get him on the phone if you need to speak with him."

"No, thank you." I smile warmly to assure her. I don't want her to worry. "I'll catch up with him later."

"I suppose Livia told everyone the exciting engagement

news?" she asks with an admirable degree of artificial excitement.

"She did. I don't suppose you know how that came about? I can only assume Zeno had something to do with it."

She clasps her hands together and takes a slow breath, her voice watered down with embarrassment. "The last I heard, Nevio was insisting on a capo's rank in order to agree to anything."

"But Z is a capo himself. He wouldn't have the power to make Nevio a capo, would he?"

*He would if he were underboss.*

Surely, he wouldn't agree to marry Ari purely to secure the position so that Nevio would marry Livia. Maybe he did agree to marry but for his own reasons. Could I have pushed him too far the other night? If he thought there was no way to keep me, would that remove the remaining barriers stopping him from marrying Ari?

My pancakes and bacon threaten to make a reappearance.

Elena shrugs helplessly. "I wouldn't think so, but I don't know for sure. He hardly said a word when he got here last night. Whatever is going on, it's consumed him almost as much as losing his father. When I heard him leave early this morning, I was so concerned I couldn't go back to sleep."

I nod shakily. "I'm sure it'll be fine."

Her sad smile tightens the vise around my heart. "Things always have a way of working out."

I say goodbye, and the second she closes the door

behind me, I pull out my phone and call Zeno. The call goes directly to voicemail, so I leave a message that I need to talk to him. I don't know what all is going on with him, but I'm starting to wish I hadn't let so much time pass since we parted on uneasy terms.

Turning to walk back home, I only take a few steps when the front door opens again behind me. I glance back to see Nevio and pause. He strolls forward, hands in his pockets, sad eyes glued to me.

"I thought I heard you." His gaze rakes over me. A look of longing tinged with remorse.

"I thought you stayed in the city."

"Drove out this morning." He takes two more slow steps until he's within my reach.

"It's early for a Saturday."

"Orders. Z says jump, and I ask how high." His hand lifts to trace the edge of my face. "You look beautiful, as ever." An apology for the awful things he said? Maybe. Too little too late? Definitely.

I take a step back. "You need to stop, Nevio."

His eyes find mine again. "It was only ever you, you know."

I'm surprised to find I believe him, in part because of what Zeno told me, but I also detect sincere regret. My relationship with him as kids and teens was probably the only genuine female connection he's ever experienced, save for his mother. I suspect he does hold a special fondness for me.

"The problem is, it would never have been *only me*." No matter how much he cares for me, his addiction would have come between us. As it is, he was having sex with my sister from the day I came back to Hardwick.

His lips pull taut in a remorseful frown. "They told you, didn't they?"

I nod.

He breathes deeply, eyes falling to the ground between us. "I suppose you would have found out eventually."

The defeat in his ragged words is heartbreaking. I want to wrap my arms around him and reassure him that everything will be okay, but that would be a lie. With the challenges he's facing, there are no guarantees, so I keep my hands and my words to myself.

Eventually, he lifts his gaze back to mine, a new earnest conviction in those mocha depths. "I *will* make an effort, though. I want you to know that I'll try to make things work with Liv. I've started back with my counselor."

"That's wonderful, Nevio. I really do wish you both the best."

He nods as though he doesn't want to part but isn't sure what else to say. "I guess I'll let you go then." His statement carries the weight of multiple meanings. He may have held a candle for me through the years, but it's time to extinguish that flame. We'll never be as close as we were as kids, but a part of me will always feel for him.

After raising my hand in goodbye, I turn toward home.

"I'm sorry, Isa," Nevio calls out. "For everything. I'm so sorry."

Twisting to look over my shoulder, I meet his tortured gaze. "I know you are, and if you ever need someone to talk to, I'm happy to listen." I feel a nagging pressure to tell him he's forgiven, but I can't find the words. His addiction doesn't excuse the way he lashed out at me. My wounds from his attack still haven't healed, and I'm not ready to fully absolve him. However, my offer to be a friend is genuine. Knowing his issues go deeper than simple insensitivity makes me want to help him rather than condemn him. I still don't think he and Livia marrying is a great idea. Nevio isn't a lost cause, but marriage to him won't be easy.

With Nevio, even friendship will have its challenges, but he's worth the effort. He's my brother—it's as simple as that.

I'm feeling hopeful when I part ways with him, and if his lopsided grin is any evidence, he feels the same.

One De Rossi relationship on the mend. One more to go.

# CHAPTER 13

As I approach home, I catch sight of a black Escalade pulling up at the front of the house. I reroute myself toward the front entry to greet whoever has arrived. I didn't think we were expecting visitors, but with six of us living under one roof, it's hard to keep track.

A glare shines on the windshield, concealing the driver, and the other windows are too tinted to see inside. Once the vehicle comes to a stop, the driver's side back seat door opens. Dressed for the boardroom, Christiano De Bellis exits the car. His steely gaze locks on me instantly like the sight of a gun trained on its target.

He's not here for my father or anyone else.

He's here for me.

Fear rushes through my veins like a river, but I don't let it show. I won't give him the satisfaction.

Forcing my posture to remain relaxed and my chin high, I do my best to broadcast confidence. If he stands close enough, he'll see the thrum of my frantic pulse at the base of my neck, but that can't be helped.

Whatever the reason for his visit, I must show strength. It's the only way to earn respect in his eyes.

"You're a beautiful woman," Christiano says, hands clasped behind his back casually. "I can understand Zeno's infatuation." He takes two steps, the start of an arcing circle around me. "We all have our dalliances, but your little fling is getting in the way of my plans. I was curious about you at first. Once I saw for myself that you were not worthy of concern, I washed my hands of the matter. However, I've just learned something ... disheartening."

I have no idea where he's going with his diatribe, so I keep my mouth shut.

"An associate of mine has gone missing, and it appears Zeno may have been involved in the disappearance. Do you know what that tells me?" He waits for me to shake my head. "That indicates Zeno is taking matters into his own hands. That tells me he's putting other people before the family. Luisa, you've been raised in the family. You must know that we can't have that. If our family is to stay strong —remain united and untouchable—the family itself must *always* come first."

I don't subscribe to his belief, but I won't argue with him. I'm not suicidal. Refusing to show fear doesn't mean I have to put my head on the chopping block. He hasn't technically asked a question, so I remain silent. He seems to prefer the sound of his own voice anyway.

"Surely you can imagine how upsetting it is when one of my top men becomes distracted not only by a woman but by some second-rate soldier's daughter."

I grit my teeth at his sneered comment.

*He wants you to lash out, Isa. Don't do it. Just don't.*

Christiano studies me as he paces. Taunts and insults me. "I spoke with him and explained my expectations. He's prepared to perform his duties and fall in line. It's time for you to remember your place as well. The question is, are you going to comply on your own, or will you need ... convincing? Because this is the only time I will ask politely."

My pulse drives too hard, too fast. I have to fight dizziness and draw a long breath in through my nose.

Would Christiano kill me to get me out of the picture? Unquestionably, yes.

Would Zeno let this man come between us? That I can't answer, and the uncertainty terrifies me. I don't want to give him up, but I'm also not prepared to die today. My only option is to give Christiano what he wants to hear and pray it's not the end of my short-lived relationship.

"I don't need convincing. If Zeno says it's over, then you have nothing to worry about." I've left myself a loophole, and he knows it.

The angry lion charges, clamping his hand around my throat in an instant. "Don't play *fucking* games with me, little girl." Up close, his eyes are black voids—a window into nothingness because there is no soul to be seen.

I gasp and nod as best as I can. "I'm sorry. I didn't mean

to." I force the sputtered words past his savage grip, pulling at his hand with frantic fingers.

He watches me squirm for an extra second, giving me one last squeeze before releasing me. I stumble backward, desperately needing space between us, and gasp for air.

Christiano looms over me menacingly. "This is the one and only time I'll tell you in unequivocal terms. Stay *the fuck* away from Zeno."

My hand rests protectively around my neck, doing little to soothe the burn within or subdue the mutinous fear taking control of me. I am no match for this man, and I hate myself for it. I want to be powerful and imposing. I want men like Christiano to think twice about intimidating me, but my strength of character only gets me so far. I am not enough threat to be of consequence.

I nod, tears heavy on my lashes. A sob claws for release, but I fight it off.

Christiano gives me one last sneer before idly returning to his car and pulling out of the driveway. Once he's gone, my knees give out, and the sobs I'd held at bay wrack my body. I can't even be relieved that he's gone when my heart threatens to collapse. Just when Zeno and I have managed to connect—to set aside our secrets and confess our feelings—the universe is going to steal it all away.

How can our sapling of a relationship ever withstand the mammoth force of Christiano's hurricane winds? He has an entire army of ruthless soldiers at his command. If we went against his orders, we could lose far more than a chance at love.

I'm on the ground, lost to desperation, when my father steps onto the porch.

"Isa? Are you okay? Was that De Bellis?" He races over and collects me in his strong arms. "Lulu, talk to me. What the hell is going on?"

"Christiano ... he wants me to stay away from Z," I hiccup through my sobs. "He ... threatened me."

"What? Why does he care?"

"He wants Z to ... marry Ari."

Dad blows out a long breath and holds me tighter. "Shit," he exhales.

We kneel together for long minutes while I compose myself. Dad is the first to break the silence.

"I need to know the truth, Isa. Do you love him?"

Lifting my gaze to his, I nod without hesitation. "I do."

"Then you need to go tell him what's going on. He needs to know. That man has loved you since you were children. I'm confident he won't let anyone keep you apart."

Not even himself? What if Christiano's threats have already swayed him? Even if they haven't, does he have enough clout of his own to go up against someone so powerful? I don't want Zeno hurt because of me.

*But are you truly willing to walk away from him out of fear?*

I don't want to let love pass me by because I'm too scared to fight for it. I couldn't live with that possibility. At the very least, I need to talk to Z. I need to see how he feels and make sure he knows what's happened.

"I could try to find him at his place in the city, but he and Christiano live in the same building. If I run into him there, he'll know I'm looking for Zeno and intentionally defying him."

"Then I'll go with you and make sure that doesn't happen."

"Dad, I can't let you get in trouble for me."

"Not your call to make, baby girl, just as I couldn't stop you from paying Mom's debt. Now, go in and get ready. We're going to the city."

# CHAPTER 14

WHILE DAD DRIVES, I TRY TO CALL Z. HE DOESN'T ANSWER, so I text to let him know I'm coming. When we arrive at Zeno's building, Dad and I put on ball caps to hide us from the security cameras—a precaution I insist upon. If Dad is going to risk himself, we will do our best to minimize being seen. Christiano made it clear he doesn't value my father in any way. If he learns Dad enabled me to see Z, the resulting punishment would be merciless.

Heads tucked, we move briskly through the lobby to the elevators. I am only somewhat relieved when we reach Zeno's door without incident because my fate is still undecided.

When I knock on Zeno's door, I'm met with silence. "He's not home, but I have the code to get in."

"You sure you'll be okay here alone?" Dad asks.

"I suppose I'll find out soon enough." I fling myself into my dad's arms. "Thank you, Daddy."

"Anything for you, Lulu. Now get inside and make sure to text me later."

"I will." I give him a weak smile, then enter the code to open the door. Once inside, I call out a hello to make sure I'm alone and set my hat and purse on the entry console. Nerves flutter and flare as I walk into the living room, keeping my lunchtime hunger at bay. I have no idea how long I'll have to wait for him to come home, so I get comfortable on the sofa. Too comfortable. I spend an hour messing around on my phone, and the next thing I know, my sleepy eyes open to the sight of Zeno standing over me.

"Oh, you're here," I murmur, a bolt of adrenaline waking me in an instant. I jump to my feet and attempt to smooth my mussed hair. "I'm sorry to intrude, but I had to talk to you."

His face darkens like a summer storm blackening the sky, sudden and intense. I hold perfectly still, worried my arrival has upset him, but his hand slowly lifts to my neck with a featherlight touch. "Is that bruising around your throat?" His words are stilted from the effort of restrained violence.

I'd been so worried about Christiano's threats, I hadn't given a thought to whether his assault had left a mark. Clearly, it had. "Christiano came by the cottage this morning," I tell him warily. I had wanted him to know, but the terrifying look on his face consumes me with worry. Not for myself. I'm scared of what Zeno might do on my behalf.

"He did this?"

I nod.

"What exactly did he say?"

"He told me to stay away from you. That he has plans for you, and I'm getting in the way." I dive into his ocean eyes and search for the truth. "Is he right, Z? Am I getting in the way? Because I don't want to be the woman who keeps you from your dreams." I don't want him to be punished because of me. "Is that why you've been so quiet? Are you having doubts?"

Z threads his hands into my hair and brings our cheeks together. "*Fuck*, no. That's not it at all. I've been spending every minute of the past few days trying to sort this shit out. Trying to fix everything without making waves. I should have reached out and explained, but I didn't want to make promises before I knew I could keep them." He pulls back and traces his thumb along my neck. "Yet again, I've fucked up. I should never have left you alone." It's a murmur to himself. An admonishment.

I pull back enough to look into his eyes and inwardly cringe at the guilt lining his face. "It's okay. I'm okay," I whisper. "I knew you had a lot to sort out, and considering the engagement news, you'd clearly been busy."

"That's definitely occupied some of my time."

"You didn't have to force the issue. She would have been fine without him."

Z takes a deep, weary breath. "Marriage will give her an easier time collecting child support and give her access to alimony when … *if* they part ways. Nevio has a way of shirking his responsibilities, and I wanted to do what I could to ensure your sister wouldn't fall victim to him more than she already has. Court orders aren't foolproof, but it should help."

I hadn't thought of it that way. "Thank you for looking out for her. I'm not sure she entirely deserves it, but I appreciate it." I recall what Elena said about Nevio's demands, and I have to ask though I'm not sure I want the answer. "Z, how did you get Nevio to agree to the marriage? Your mom said he was asking to be made a capo."

"He would like that to happen, but I don't have the ability to promote him myself and wouldn't even if I could. He's not trustworthy enough. Instead, I gave him the next best thing—control of his finances. After dealing with his issues for years, my dad decided to put Nevio's money in a trust to keep it protected—the money our parents had accrued for him. His own earnings are untouched but fractional compared to the trust. It pissed him off to no end that he wasn't given control over his own assets. The trust was one of the many issues that came between my father and him. Upon Dad's death, I became the trustee with the power to allocate the funds. And the power to dissolve the trust."

"You gave him his money?"

"I did. Or ... I will, once he's gone through with the wedding. He may be an addict, but drugs or gambling aren't an issue. I've had to meet with our attorney and the accountant and make plans for the transition. I've also stipulated that Nevio has to continue sessions with his counselor."

"He mentioned that. I ran into him this morning."

His brows rise. "You've had a busy day already."

"I have." The words are but a breath squeezed from seizing lungs. Anticipation unfurls from deep in my chest, launching my pulse into a breakneck rhythm.

It's time to say what I've come here to say.

My eyes follow my trembling fingers as they touch the broad chest before me. An uncertain, tentative touch seeking connection. Strength. Reassurance.

"Z, I came here today to tell you about Christiano, but that's not all. I want you to know—I *need* you to know—that I love you ... so much." I can barely speak past the ball of emotion lodged in my throat, but I force myself to go on because my feelings are too important to go unsaid. "I've adored you since I was a little girl with scraped knees. Even our years apart couldn't erase my feelings for you. And the reason I needed to know if you'll refuse Christiano's wishes isn't because I'm impatient or demanding. It's because my love for you is too consuming for me to share you. I could never be the woman on the side, even if a relationship with Ari was purely superficial. I simply couldn't. It would devastate me. So, before my heart is irrevocably bound to you, I need to know if there's a chance for us. A real chance for it to be just you and me."

I'm relieved to have the truth out in the open before he even says a word. I love Zeno. I love him so deeply that my heart beats to his rhythm. I won't degrade that love or myself by relegating either of us to the shadows. I am worth so much more.

Z lifts my chin with the gentle touch of his fingers. "There's more than a chance." His penetrating stare is unflinching. "I'm going to make it happen. You were right to demand an answer, and it wasn't fair of me to put you in that position. The answer should have been yes. Unequivocally, yes. The only reason I didn't say it then was because I didn't know how to make it happen. That's what has taken a majority of my time over the past few days. I want to make things right with you in every way I can so that when I put my ring on your finger, nothing is left to come between us." Z lowers until his lips to ghost over mine. "I love you, Luisa Banetti, down to the darkest depths of my soul."

When our lips finally connect, the kiss sears his name onto the surface of my heart, claiming it as his own. A permanent reminder of the bond that has always existed between us. Not even years or miles or hate could sever the connection. Each has tried and failed. Our need for one another is eternal.

Z lifts me, coaxing my legs around his waist, and walks us back to his bedroom. The shades are lowered with only a small panel of light left at the bottom of each to illuminate the room. Plenty for me to see the inked lines of his tattoos and every dip and swell of his muscled body as I remove his clothes. He does the same for me, taking care to worship each new stretch of exposed skin with his touch.

"I've fucked up with you more times than should be humanly possible, yet here you are, next to me, offering your forgiveness and love. It's beyond my comprehension." Zeno walks us backward until my legs press against the bed, then reaches behind me and yanks the covers down.

I ease back onto the cool sheets, my eyes never leaving

his. "We were victim to circumstances beyond our control. That's no one's fault."

He prowls over me, caging my body beneath his. "Not anymore. Now I'm in control, and nothing is going to come between us again." His mouth descends on my nipple, twirling his tongue and grazing the taut peak with his teeth until I'm writhing with need, then he switches to the other side.

Reaching between us, I wrap my hand around the velvety softness of his cock. When I squeeze his length, he hisses with pleasure. The sound adds fuel to my fire, and soon, my core is weeping with need.

Z nips at the side of my breast before pulling upright and reaching for the nightstand. I expect him to come away with a condom, but instead, he rips open a small box and plucks out something small and pink that he slips on his fingers—a vibrator device made specifically for the clit. He then grabs two pillows from where they've scattered around us and has me lift my hips. I watch his every movement with rapt fascination. He hasn't struck me as the type of man who uses toys, but I'm extremely fond of my vibrator, so this new insight has me giddy with anticipation.

Once he has me where he wants me, he squirts gel onto the pink device then brings it to my center, allowing me to adjust to its bumpy texture before turning it on. His eyes devour my every movement. Each gasp and arch. When he clicks on the power, I buck from the sudden blast of sensation.

"Oh, *God*, Zeno." My eyes roll back as I absorb the pleasure coursing through my veins.

I'm used to the intense sensation of a vibrator, but it's different when someone else is controlling the device. Every touch is magnified, and every pause spikes my pulse with anticipation. The vulnerability of my position is intensely erotic. The trust and uncertainty battling one another cause a cataclysmic storm to brew inside me.

"I love to see you splayed open for me, your perfect pink cunt begging for my touch."

Z lifts his fingers away, giving me time to breathe, then resumes his systematic onslaught, sliding the silicon vibrations from one side to the other. He is transfixed at the sight of me. I try to watch him because I'm equally enraptured by the sight of him, but his ministrations are too distracting.

Eventually, he removes his hand to guide himself inside me. He remains upright on his knees, eyes glued to where our bodies become one.

I assume he's done with the toy, but I'm wrong. Once he's sheathed himself fully inside me, muscles straining with need, his fingers return to resume their delicious torture. He uses his free hand to clutch my hip while he thrusts inside me.

I've never felt such a barrage of sensations.

The vibrations.

His pounding cock.

They unite to overwhelm my brain. I can't focus on any one thing, giving my body over to sensation. I clutch the sheets beneath me as white light threatens the edge of my vision. My breaths become shallow pants. My stomach tightens, and my legs begin to spasm.

"*There it is. Z, yes, don't stop.*"

"Oh, *fuck yes*, Isa. Squeeze me. You feel so fucking good." He thrusts harder and faster, triggering that perfect explosion like liquid jet fuel igniting in my veins. The fiery pleasure swells from my center until it fills every molecule of my being, and I am splitting at the seams.

The orgasm is too violent to contain. It bursts from my throat in a primal scream that leaves me ragged and raw—the discarded shell of a shotgun blast, still scalding from the explosion. I find my breath as I float back to earth. Slowly, my body and mind reunite.

Zeno eases in and out of me, giving me time to soak in the sensation. I hardly notice when he removes the pillows from beneath me—not until his body is flush with mine.

I open my eyes to lock with his. Open my heart to make room for him.

He waits until he sees that I'm back with him, connected and ready. Then he makes love to me.

Face-to-face.

Heart-to-heart.

Each thrust is a promise. Each kiss an oath. I have no remaining reason to question him because his devotion is absolute, and he proves as much by worshiping my body with infinite care. When his release overtakes him, I clutch him against me, swearing an oath of my own to return his love with the same ardent ferocity.

# CHAPTER 15

"What made you decide to stop pushing me away?" I lie next to Zeno in the preternatural twilight of his room. He's pulled the sheets over us and drawn me into his side, his arm holding me securely against him. I've tried to keep my thoughts at bay and simply enjoy our moment together, but I've never been good at not thinking.

"I started to realize how much I was hurting the both of us. Through the years, I'd told myself that you saw me as an annoyance and nothing more, so my harsh rebukes were only damaging to me. But seeing you day after day— witnessing the way you reacted to me—I began to wonder if the harm I was doing was outweighed by the good. Yes, I had managed to keep you away from Hardwick and my brother. But what if there was another way I could keep you safe from Nevio? What if you were mine instead?

Once the thought took root, I couldn't escape it. I wanted you more than anything, but I knew there was a strong possibility I'd ruined my chances of that ever happening."

"I was so angry with you, especially that night you admitted your feelings."

"I could tell. I was certain after I left that I'd done too much damage to overcome. If there was any hope at all, it lay in the truth. That one sliver of a chance—the hope that a confession might earn your forgiveness—was worth spilling my secrets. Even if we didn't end up together, I hoped to at least keep you from hating me."

I mull over my next words because I'm not sure how they'll be received. "Z, it's not my call to make, but I want you to consider telling your mom and maybe even Nevio the truth. Secrets are insidious. They fester and rot everything they touch. And besides, secrets always end up exposed in the end. Better to control how the information surfaces than clean up after a bomb drops."

Zeno grunts. "I'm not sure I agree, but I'll consider it." He rolls us so that I'm on my back and he's on his side, looming over me. "And what about you? Hmm? Are you going to fess up as well?"

I search his face, relieved to sense an element of playfulness even though I'm unsure what he's getting at. "What do you mean?"

He lowers his mouth to graze his teeth over my jawline. "I mean ... this isn't the first time you've had an orgasm in my bed." His voice is liquid caramel, hot and sticky as it coats my skin.

He knows. *Holy shit, he knows.*

My heart jackhammers against my ribs. I'd fingered myself on his bed while I was staying at his apartment, freaking out over what I'd let myself do, but I had convinced myself he'd never know. That my moment of weakness would stay buried forever. How could he know unless ... "You have cameras?" I shriek in horror.

"I do," he purrs. "I don't normally check the footage, but after our awkward dinner at Christiano's, I wanted to check in on you. When I saw you creep to my room, I had to keep watching. It was the most erotic, incredible thing I've ever witnessed. That's why I came over the next day. I couldn't think of anything but you. That was the moment I realized I might actually have a chance with you."

"I was out of line," I breathe, my embarrassment transforming to something more seductive. Something sensual and exhilarating.

*"You were fucking perfect."*

His unabashed desire for me stokes life into body parts that had felt spent minutes before. My breasts feel heavy with need, and my hips flex in search of friction against my now throbbing center.

"Just like that," he murmurs. "I want to know exactly how much you need me."

I lift my eyes to his and smirk. "Oh, yeah? Well, how about this?" In a bout of playfulness, I roll us so that he's on his back, and I'm gleefully on top of him, thighs spread wide on either side of him.

When I raise above him victoriously, Z thrusts his head back into the pillow and howls with laughter. It's the most exultant, incredible thing I've ever heard. His laugh should be memorialized as a national treasure, too rare and precious to waste. Though, if I have any say in the matter, he'll be laughing much more in the future.

While his abs flex and ripple with his laughter, I ease myself lower until my face is inches from the thick head of his shaft. My eyes lift to lock with his, and all levity evaporates. Zeno watches me raptly as my tongue extends. When I make contact and lick his full length, veins already bulging from his renewed erection, his entire body shivers.

I can taste myself on him. That's not something I would have thought I'd like, but with Z, tasting the evidence of our passion means so much more than a bodily fluid. It's the bond of two people who have always belonged to one another.

Taking him into my mouth, I suck him deep into my throat, humming my satisfaction. His moan and staggered breaths are ample reward, spurring me on to see if I can make him mindless with need. When his hand clutches my head, I think I've nearly got him, but instead, he coaxes my lips from his and flips us. He wields his strength with such sudden force that I gasp and am on my back beneath him before I know what's happened.

"My turn," he growls, clasping my wrists in one of his hands.

I am powerless beneath him. A willing victim to whatever sublime torture he wishes to inflict.

Sensing my eagerness, Z flashes a villainous grin before laying siege to my body. We spend hours together in bed, exploring and talking until my stomach growls in protest. I never did eat lunch. Z heats a pasta dish, which we eat out on his balcony, enjoying the sprawling night views of the city. When our stomachs are full, exhaustion descends upon us both. We head back to bed, and I'm asleep in an instant, peacefully engulfed in Zeno's embrace.

We don't rouse until well into Sunday morning. Waking next to Z makes my chest flutter with happiness, especially when I feel his hand resting on my forearm. I've rolled away from him in the night, but he's found a way to maintain contact as though he needs that connection even in his sleep.

I shift onto my side. Z's eyelids lift at the movement.

"Morning," I say with a soft smile.

"Mmm..." His chest vibrates with a morning purr. He pulls me against him and nuzzles his face into my hair. "What time is it?"

"Late, I think—maybe around ten. I probably need to have some breakfast and get back home." I don't want to intrude on his day, and I have my own chores to get back to.

"I wasn't planning to go back to Hardwick until tomorrow. Why don't you stay until then?"

"Because I have to work tomorrow?"

"No, you don't. As of this moment, you're fired."

I twist until I can see his face behind me, trying to discern his meaning. "Z, I need that job. It may be awkward for me to work for you, but it's not forever."

Zeno huffs. "Have you checked your accounts lately?"

"No." My face scrunches with confusion. "Why?"

"Because you've got plenty of money. What's mine is yours. Besides, you never should have been put in the position to use your school money. Now you can call St. Joseph's tomorrow morning and change your status back to active. You can start in the fall like you'd planned." He pulls me back snug against him and whispers close to my ear. "You agreed to be mine. That won't always be easy, but there are certain ... perks."

I can't say that I'm stunned because it makes sense for him to help me, but I've never expected handouts. With everything so uncertain between us, I hadn't even allowed myself to explore the what-ifs of a happily ever after.

My mind begins to race with possibilities. "I wonder if that girl still needs a roommate." The question is for myself, though I murmur it aloud. If I'm going to return to school, I'll need to find another living situation.

"Fuck, no. You'll live here with me. Once you graduate, you can decide where we go from there."

"Move in?" I balk. "Z, we've been on exactly *one* date. Don't you think that might be rushing things?"

The gorgeous, cryptic man moves on top of me, pressing his hard length into the junction of my thighs. "I told you my definition of rushing might be different than yours. We've known each other too long and been through too much to follow some arbitrary timetable. I'm not missing out on a single opportunity to be near you."

I gasp at the coiling tension stirring in my belly. "I suppose I can manage to wake up like this every morning."

The corners of my mouth hook upward playfully. Who am I to say no to such a generous offer?

Logic tells me rushing things could lead to problems, but I can't name one concrete objection aside from shoulds or mights. We're moving fast, but maybe that's the perfect speed for us.

Zeno's victorious grin fills my heart to bursting. Then he slips beneath the covers, his eyes blazing with a desire to fill other parts of me.

By the time we finally make it out to the kitchen, breakfast becomes brunch, and I'm showered but starving. Z cooks pancakes while I cut up a few pieces of fruit. He's wearing a low-slung pair of pajama pants, and from behind, I've got a perfect view of the dimpled indents directly above his ass. I'm amazed at how even the most random of body parts are sexy as hell when it comes to Zeno.

We discuss our plans for the day over breakfast. I agree to spend the day with him if he agrees to get me back to my parents' house by evening. There's only so long a girl can go without a change of underwear. Z has generously kept me underwear-free to help in that cause, but the time has come.

I wipe down the counter as Z loads the last dish into the dishwasher when his doorbell rings. Our gazes collide, mine wide with terror, his steely with determination. There's no guarantee that it's Christiano at the door, but we both know the odds are good.

"He can't know I'm here," I hiss quietly.

Zeno nods. "Agreed. Go back to the bedroom, and I'll take care of it."

He doesn't have to tell me twice. I take off for the hallway, screeching to a stop when I spot my cap and purse in the front entry. Padding on the balls of my feet as quietly as possible, I detour to snag my things, then disappear around the corner. A voice in my head urges me to hide in the closet, but I don't give in to the temptation. Instead, I plaster myself to the hallway wall and strain my ears to hear what's being said.

"...decided to take the day off." Zeno's voice echoes back to me.

My pulse is so loud in my ears that I have to make a concentrated effort to calm myself just so I can hear.

"We all need a day here and there." Christiano's voice comes closer as though he's slowly wandering into the living area. "I won't interrupt you for long, but I need to have a quick word."

"You know you're welcome anytime." Z's tone is easy, but he doesn't invite his boss to stay. I wonder if that's normal. I don't want Christiano around any longer than necessary, but I don't want to make him suspicious either.

"The time has come for me to name a successor to your father. You know I've always had high hopes for you, yet lately, you've given me a reason for concern. I'm done dancing around the subject and watching you piss on my generosity." His comment makes me think that his claim about already talking to Zeno was garbage, as I'd suspected. He was posturing and only now bringing up the subject.

"I'm sorry to hear you feel that way. I've never meant to upset you."

"It's been understood for years that you and Ari are the future of this organization. You know it, and so does everyone of any importance. How do you think it makes me look when you disrespect my wishes and reject my daughter for some penniless housekeeper whose father couldn't muster more than a soldier's rank? You say you didn't mean to upset me, but how else am I to receive such a slight?"

Several heartbeats pass before Zeno responds. "Would you really want that type of marriage for Ari or myself when neither of us desires a relationship with one another?" His voice is tight but respectful. He's trying his best to reason with Christiano.

"What is this? *The* fucking *Bachelor*? We're not in the business of fucking love connections, Zeno. Surely, you're not that deluded."

"Surely, our organization has moved past the dark ages when a man has to bind himself to a woman he doesn't love out of obligation." Z's clipped response is unquestionably aggressive, and it terrifies me.

Why the hell had I ever wanted Z to stand up to his boss? Now that the conversation is unfolding, I'm reconsidering everything I said. I want our freedom to be together, but can that be achieved without the risk of death?

Judging by Christiano's vicious reply, the threat is very real.

"You need to grow the fuck up and learn how this

world works," he spits. "Status is everything. Marriage has never been anything but a strategy for survival, and that's just as true today as it was then. If you can't see that, then you're a greater fool than I realized." He pauses, and I envision the two men locked in a vicious stare. "You want to run this family one day? You know my terms. Either put the family first like you swore to do, or watch as you lose everything. I want a final answer by the end of the week." Clacking footsteps charge toward the door, which slams upon his departure.

I melt against the wall. The flood of adrenaline leaving my system drains all the strength from my body. When I'm finally steady enough to go in search of Z, I find him staring out the living room windows. I approach from behind and wrap my arms around his middle, pressing my cheek to his bare back.

"What are we going to do?" I ask weakly.

"We're going to throw an engagement party for Nevio and Livia."

Confused, I peer around him and study his reflection in the plate glass. Not an ounce of worry, only resolute determination. I desperately wish I shared his confidence. If it were only our lives at stake, I could possibly dredge up more bravado, but our choices will affect everyone we care about. Christiano isn't the type of man to forgive and forget. If we jump in the ring with him, we have to be prepared for a fight to the death.

# CHAPTER 16

"*Engaged?*" I gape at my older sister, whose tear-filled brown eyes are as joyful as I've ever seen them. "I was only gone for one night!" I came upstairs in search of Gia the minute Zeno dropped me off at home. I'd wanted to tell her everything that had gone on, but it turns out she had news to share as well.

Gia laughs with a sniffle and gazes down at the exquisite diamond on her finger. "I know! It's all happened so quickly."

"I suppose you've sorted out the whole debacle with him disappearing then?" I hadn't pushed for an explanation. I'd been preoccupied, and she'd hardly been home since Carter came back from the city.

"Definitely. He explained everything—that his feelings for me were growing, but he was worried he would be strapping me down with kids when I'm younger than him. He thought he would be doing me a favor to leave and admitted that he didn't handle the situation well. When I told him how heartbroken I was to think of losing him *and* the kids, that sealed everything." She smiles at me with a grin that could end wars and heal the sick.

"Gia, honey, I'm so happy for you!" I hug my sister close.

"I better go down and tell the others. I wanted to tell you first."

"You haven't told them yet? Mom is going to wet herself. Come on, let's do this."

Finding out yet another daughter will be marrying money manages to bring Mom out of her divorce-laden funk. While she doesn't actually wet herself, she does spill half a glass of rosé down her shirt. We spend the next hour sitting at the table daydreaming about wedding plans and giggling over wine. It's the perfect release after an emotionally exhausting weekend. When we finally crawl into bed, I'm asleep within minutes.

THE FOLLOWING week is spent making arrangements for the engagement party to be held Saturday night. The event is larger than I initially expected. Z's guest list includes about forty people—the Bishops, Larsons, and several important families from work. Of course, Savio, Christiano, and Ari have been invited as well. I don't know what exactly Z has planned for Christiano or how an engagement party plays into those plans. I also haven't pushed for answers. Hell, maybe the party has nothing to do with Christiano. I have no idea. Even if I did ask, I get the sense Zeno wouldn't give me any answers. All I know is the planning keeps me busy, and I appreciate not having time to worry.

I try to explain to Mom about my new relationship with Zeno and how I'll no longer be working at Hardwick without her jumping to conclusions, but I might as well try to contain the ocean. She is ecstatic and loses all pretense of worry over her divorce. Mom can't imagine a scenario where she struggles when three of her daughters will be wealthy even though she has no claim to any money. I have too much going on to force the subject at the moment. It's a bridge we'll cross when the time comes. For now, I let her have her excitement. It'll make things easier for Dad to get his freedom.

Each day I work on party plans, and each night I spend in Zeno's bed. Elena's room is on the opposite end of the house, so that isn't an issue. I find that mornings with her brighten my days. She is more discreet with her emotions than my mother, but even she can't hide her joy at seeing Zeno and me together. And the more I learn about Elena and the De Rossi family, the more happiness I think she deserves. It's easy to assume someone with so much money must lead an enchanted life, but that isn't always the case. Elena's been handed her fair share of struggles. I'm pleased that her tides have turned.

When Saturday finally arrives, I can't shake the nerves that constrict my muscles into angry knots. The mere anticipation of Christiano's presence drives my pulse to a breaking point. He doesn't want me anywhere near Zeno, and I'll be seated next to the man at a Hardwick dinner party. I can't imagine a scenario where that goes down well, no matter how many times Z assures me everything will be fine.

To combat those insidious insecurities and fears, I select a black halter dress that makes me feel invincible. Thick smoky eye shadow is my war paint, and chandelier earrings that dangle over my bare shoulders act as my armor. Blood-red patent heels serve as my weapon in this battle of power. I want every advantage I can get when going up against someone as ruthless and powerful as Christiano De Bellis.

The party invitation stated seven, though a cocktail hour will precede the actual dinner. Savio shows up early and begins the parade of arrivals at half after six. I'm delighted to see Grace arrive with her parents and learn that she decided to make an unexpected visit home for the weekend. When I ask if she knew Ari would be here, she looks genuinely surprised.

"She told me she was doing something with her dad, but I didn't realize they would be here at Hardwick. That's part of the reason I came home because she was going to be busy all weekend." She looks a touch hurt. I imagine she's wondering why Ari wouldn't tell her she'd be at a Hardwick dinner party, and I have no answers for her.

"I'm sure she just didn't consider that your parents might also be invited. This probably feels like any other work function for her."

"You're probably right." She smiles and nods without much conviction. "Mom told me about Gia's engagement as well. I can't believe how fast everything is happening, but I'm so happy for her."

"She is beside herself. At least that's one engagement I can truly celebrate."

Grace leans in conspiratorially, though no one is standing close. "How is Livia? Has she been to a doctor yet?"

"No, she hasn't. She's doing well, though, aside from a nasty case of morning sickness that makes it hard to gloat about her engagement. I don't feel as bad for her as I probably should. So far, she seems fine tonight. She's been waving her hand around since she arrived, making sure her ring is prominently displayed."

"And Nevio?" Her eyes cut to where the couple stands talking to some of Zeno's associates.

"He's playing his part well enough." And anyone who knows him well can see his act for exactly what it is. Nevio wears his heart on his sleeve. If he felt any true joy, the room would glow from the energy he'd radiate.

When I turn my eyes back to Grace, she's eyeing me curiously.

"And what about you? How are things with Z?"

My gaze drifts to him. In less than a second, his eyes are on me as well, as though he can sense my attention. "Things are good," I say with a grin, turning back to Grace. "Things are really good."

*Assuming Christiano doesn't murder us both.*

Grace takes my hand and squeezes. "That's so

wonderful to hear." Her smile wavers at the sight of something over my shoulder.

I turn to see Ari enter the room.

*They're here. Oh, God. They're here.*

Except, they're not. Ari is alone.

I stare at the front door and wait for Christiano to make his appearance, but it doesn't happen.

"Um, I'm going to chat with Ari, okay?" Grace asks distractedly.

"Of course, you go." I couldn't possibly concentrate anyway.

Minutes tick by until seven has come and gone. Christiano is noticeably absent.

"Excuse me, everyone," Zeno calls out above the din of voices. "Now that the sun isn't beating down so heavily, I invite you out to the plaza in the back where we will be dining. I have a quick matter to attend to, and then I'll join you shortly." He nods to Savio, and the two start in the direction of Zeno's office.

I'm curious about their conference and whether it has anything to do with Christiano's absence, but an answer will have to wait. I join everyone outside and use the opportunity to ask Ari about her father. She assures me he's coming and was held up in a meeting with someone.

I don't know if I feel better or worse. The uncertainty of him not showing made me anxious, yet I don't want him here either.

Sounds like it's time for a cocktail.

I mosey toward the drink table and spy Z through his office window. He's pacing but not in an overly agitated manner. I can't see his face because a dark screen is halfway down the window to ward off the afternoon sun. His expression might have helped me discern what's going on, but it's hidden from view. Instead, I down a large gulp of wine and return to visiting with friends.

Elena hired a company to create an elegant dinner setting complete with white lights crisscrossing overhead and bouquets of white flowers all around. Five round tables are fully set in the center of the flagstone plaza covered in crisp white tablecloths reaching down to the ground. It's a touch warm out but not insufferable. Had the weather not cooperated, we would have changed plans and hosted inside, but the plaza is preferrable with its lake views.

I mingle with the guests, spending most of my time talking to people I know and leave Elena and my dad to schmooze with those I don't. A half hour later, Zeno and Savio emerge from the house and join the party. I make my way to Z as quickly as I can without drawing suspicion.

"Is everything okay?"

His hand cups the back of my neck, bringing me close to kiss my temple. "Everything is just fine."

The gears in my brain spring free of their mechanism and clatter to the floor, leaving me speechless. I'd been fully prepared for Zeno to treat me like a casual acquaintance in front of his Mafia associates. Never in a million years did I think he'd make such an overtly possessive gesture in front of everyone. In front of Christiano's cronies. His touch … that kiss … everyone will know, and I get the sense that's his plan. He's claiming me for everyone to see, and for those who weren't here, word will quickly spread.

I'm terrified and thrilled all at once.

I search for my voice as Zeno's hand drifts down to the small of my back. His branding touch sears my skin in the best way imaginable.

"I suppose you've noticed that Christiano hasn't arrived?" I ask breathlessly.

Z draws my gaze to his. "You have nothing to worry about. I promise. Now, let me introduce you to some of my associates."

I nod and allow him to lead the way. We mingle together for a short while longer before Zeno announces the start of dinner, and everyone takes their seats. Z and I sit with Elena, Nevio, Livia, my parents, and Marca. Mom is playing nice with Dad, though she seats Marca between them. I'd prefer to sit with Gia or Grace and avoid the awkwardness at my designated table, but as the host, Z needs to sit with the guests of honor, and he insisted I sit with him when we were arranging seat placards this morning.

I adore his proud ownership of our relationship, but it's come without explanation. I'm not the type to go along with things blindly. It takes all my patience and all the newly developed trust I have in Zeno to set aside my anxiety.

Christiano doesn't show for dinner, nor does he arrive in time for dessert. After we raise our glasses in toast to the happy couple, Ari approaches our table and whispers to Z.

He takes out his phone and places a call that doesn't appear to be answered. Then another.

Goose bumps rise along my arms, despite the summer temperatures. The concern on their faces tells me all I need to know. Something's wrong.

Zeno excuses himself to talk to the man he'd first introduced to me before dinner. Savio joins them, and the three men exchange a few words before excusing themselves. I instinctively stand and walk to the group along with Ari.

"Z, what's going on?" I pull him aside and try to look casual so as not to alert the other guests.

"We can't get ahold of Christiano or his men. We're going to his place to make sure there's not a problem."

"Is Ari going?"

"Yes, it's her father."

"Then I'm going too." The words are out before I've thought them through. A week of uncertainty has worn through my patience. I have to know what's going on.

Z frowns at the conviction in my eyes and glances at Ari. "Okay. Let me tell Mom what's going on, and we'll go."

We receive a few curious glances from the guests, but we try to look unbothered as we make our exit. Ari and I squeeze in the back seat of Z's Range Rover with Savio while their associate sits in front with Zeno. When we pull up at the De Bellis mansion, all is quiet. The men step out, pulling guns from thin air and instructing Ari and me to stay in the car.

I've never seen Ari look so anxious. She's always so composed that a bouncing knee and white knuckles speak volumes.

"It's going to be okay," I assure her, clasping my hand over hers.

"When he didn't show up, I called, but he didn't answer. I tried his bodyguards, but they didn't answer either. That's never happened before."

"Could they have gone somewhere without phone service?"

She chews on the inside of her cheek as her wide blue eyes connect with mine. "I don't know," she whispers like a lost child.

Minutes later, Zeno marches toward the car. Ari scrambles to open the door, and I slip out of the car behind her.

"What's happened?" she asks.

His piercing gaze touches me before he places both hands on Ari's arms. "There's been an attack," he says calmly. His voice is surprisingly soothing. "I'm so sorry, Ari, but your father didn't make it. We've called an ambulance, but he's already gone."

Her chest expands with the news, rocking her body backward like the ricochet of a gun.

Christiano was a monster, but he was also her father. Her only parent. I can't imagine what she's feeling.

I push forward and envelop her in a hug. "Oh, God. Ari, I'm so sorry."

Her body trembles beneath me, her hands slowly rising to cling to me. "I need to see him," she whispers.

I pull back and look at her, then at Z. "I'm not sure that's a good idea."

"Ari, you don't want to do that," Z chimes in.

Ari sidesteps me toward Zeno with surprising ferocity,

jabbing his chest with a manicured finger. "I'm going to see him." Her voice is absolute. She will not tolerate being challenged.

Z raises his hands in defeat.

Ari starts toward the house, and I follow in her wake.

"Where the hell do you think you're going?" Z barks, rushing to catch up with me.

"With her. I'm not letting her go in there alone."

He spews a litany of curses but doesn't fight me. It's a good thing, too, because I've shifted into mother-bear mode. Ari needs a woman's strength with her, and I'm not going to abandon her. If she needs to see her father, then I'm going with her.

Her footsteps slow as we enter the house, but she doesn't stray from her mission. We pass an enormous man lying in a pool of blood. I remember seeing him outside the elevator at Christiano's city apartment. He may have been huge, but a bullet to the chest ended his life as quickly as it would any other man.

Savio and the fifth member of our party stand in the kitchen, both on their phones. A second body lies at their feet. Ari and I slowly make our way over. Our heels clack against the marble floors, echoing throughout the cavernous room. The house is eerily silent. I've never seen a tornado or experienced its aftermath, but this strange helplessness can't be far off the feeling. The quiet insignificance of stumbling across a disaster after the fact.

Christiano is on his stomach. It's a small mercy. We can't see his face, but his finely suited form is unmistakable. Like the other man, blood pools beneath him in a viscous puddle.

Ari and I come to a stop some twenty feet away from him. I'm locked in a trance until I hear her stilted breaths beside me. Tears stream down her cheeks, and her face is as white as the marble floors at our feet.

"Come here, honey." I pull her into my arms and move her away from the sight of her father.

Savio ends his call and walks to Zeno. "The others are coming from your place."

"Cops will love that," Z murmurs. "A whole crew of people fucking up their crime scene."

"What are we going to tell them?" the other man asks.

"What we know," Z answers. "He was meeting with someone before joining us at the party. When he didn't show, we came looking for him."

I start to process what the men are saying and am struck by how unusual it is that the police were called. The Mafia likes to handle its matters privately. But this was the boss. Maybe that makes a difference.

The whole thing is so unusual. What are the odds that Christiano is murdered when Zeno was in the process of defying the man? It's awfully coincidental. Had he hired a hitman or maybe enabled an enemy to do his dirty work for him? Both options would create loose ends that worried me. And what about Ari? Would he have sent someone when she possibly could have been hurt as well?

I'm not sure what to think. Z said he'd handle Christiano, and it makes sense that killing him might have been the only way, but I had intentionally ignored that possibility. It's such a dangerous proposition. Killing Aldo was one thing, but killing the boss of the Giordano family is far riskier.

Within minutes, several familiar faces from our dinner party appear at the house. Each looks more merciless than the last. How could these men be one and the same as the smiling revelers at Hardwick? Their personalities had flipped like two sides of a coin.

"Jesus Christ," one spits. "Looks like a hit. Who the fuck would do this?"

"You check the cameras yet?" another asks.

"Turned off," Savio confirms. "Whoever was behind it knew what they were doing."

"So, we got no witnesses and no film. We can't even go for retribution if we don't have any fuckin' clue who's behind it."

Tension swells in the room around us.

"That's not our only problem," the first man says. "He hadn't even named a new underboss. Now the whole organization will be fucking chaos."

The others grunt their agreement.

"Actually," Savio replies. "Christiano spoke to me this morning. He was ready to announce that Zeno would be his next in command."

All eyes, including mine, swivel to Z.

"It's true," Ari chimes in, her voice empty. "He was telling me before I went to the party tonight that he planned to announce Zeno's promotion at dinner."

Christiano had chosen Zeno as underboss? But how? Why would he have changed his mind? And if Savio knew, had he not told Z? Was that why they'd spoken in Zeno's office before dinner? If so, why hadn't he told me when I asked what was going on?

I'm so lost, but there's no time for confusion. Sirens quickly fill the air around us.

"We can discuss this later," Zeno orders. "If any of you prefer not to give a statement, I suggest you head out the back. The rest of us should step out front."

Everyone follows his instructions without question. We're there giving statements for almost two hours. When the authorities finally release us, we take Ari back to Hardwick with us and get her set up in a guest room. Her father's house is now a crime scene, and she's too exhausted to drive back to the city. Fortunately, they allow her to collect the overnight bag she'd brought with her and a few items from the house.

Once we've updated Elena and seen to Ari, Z and I retreat to his bedroom. We sit on the bed and address a barrage of missed texts and calls until Z tosses both our phones onto the dresser and wordlessly leads me to the bathroom. He turns on the shower, then helps me from my dress. I step into the steaming water while he undresses, then wrap my arms around his middle when he joins me.

We stand silently in the spray of water for long minutes, absorbing strength from one another.

"Z, do you think we could be in danger?" The question has been haunting me all evening. If Zeno wasn't responsible for Christiano's death, then someone else was. Would that person want the new underboss dead as well?

He lathers soap in his hands and massages my shoulders, drawing a moan from deep in my throat.

"Danger? That's inherent in my line of work, but no, we're not in any imminent danger." The smooth and relaxed baritone tenor of his voice is reassuring and confident.

I lift my gaze and study his face, searching for answers. "Were you responsible for Christiano's death?"

"What makes you ask that?" His voice grows husky, and his hands trail down to graze around the outside of my breasts. When his thumbs pluck at my nipples, a bolt of lightning zings straight to my core.

I gasp and arch, pressing my chest into his capable hands. "I don't know. It just seems awfully convenient."

"Maybe from our perspective, but we weren't the only ones who had a problem with Christiano."

*That's true.*

Z rinses us and lifts me into his arms, leaning my back against the shower wall. I gasp at the shock of cold. His lips slant over mine, stealing my remaining breath. When he pulls away, I open my mouth to ask another question, but he silences me with a single thrust, driving deep inside me.

"No more questions." The command is ragged and absolute.

I don't argue. I can't. Not while his cock is melting my insides.

Zeno's hunger for me is palpable, my thirst for him insatiable. We grope and thrust and devour one another as though these will be our last seconds together, but instead, this is only the beginning.

"Now nothing can come between us," Z pants between thrusts. His thoughts must have taken him to the same place as mine.

I squeeze my legs tightly around his hips, trying to guide myself toward that precipice I sense clamoring in the distance. Zeno fucks me with savage intensity. It is all I can do to hang on like a palm bending with the winds of a hurricane. I don't normally come from penetration alone, but his punishing thrusts slap his body against my clit in a way that stokes a fire in my veins. My orgasm barrels into me. I claw at his back, unable to stop myself. Zeno doesn't seem to mind. His release comes seconds after mine, a roaring animalistic fury. He pants and clings to me, his movement slowing as our bodies normalize.

When my feet lower to the ground, Z has to keep me upright while my legs recover.

"I've got you."

And he does. Mind, body, and soul.

# CHAPTER 17

I'm alone in Zeno's bed when I wake the next morning. It's still early, but he's already gone. After the events of last night, I imagine his days will be busy for some time.

I decided to search for him, hoping he didn't have to leave for the city. I slip on one of his undershirts and a pair of pajama pants I brought over a few days earlier. After giving my teeth a good scrubbing, I head downstairs. As I reach the last couple of steps, Zeno's voice resonates from the sitting area around the corner. My initial reaction is relief that he's still here, but then his words register.

"I never thought I'd tell you this." His voice is gentle but grave. Is he talking to Elena or someone on the phone? Whatever he's about to say is serious. Anyone with any decency would retrace their steps and allow him a private conversation. I am apparently not that person. Instead, I creep closer to the wall separating us and shamelessly eavesdrop.

"I know about your relationship with Antonio Banetti. I've known for a long time." He's talking to his mother, listening to my suggestion and telling her the truth.

I'm so incredibly proud of him and touched that he took my advice to heart.

Silence follows his admission. Elena must murmur something. I don't hear her, but Z continues as though responding to her.

"It is. I was so angry at first, but over the years, I've realized that relationships are complex. Rarely are things one-sided and as simple as black and white. I know who you are, so I trust that you had your reasons for what happened."

"I never wanted you to think poorly of your father. You adored everything about him."

"Maybe more than I should have," Z admits. "No one is perfect, and we'd all be better off accepting that."

"I'd like to explain a little if you're willing to listen."

Z is quiet, but he must nod or give some assent for her to continue.

"When I agreed to marry your father, I was young. We didn't know each other well, but I thought I knew enough that we'd be happy together. I didn't learn until a few years later that he'd been in a relationship with someone else for many years."

My suspicions were right. Not only did Silvano have another woman but Elena also knew about the relationship. I can't imagine how painful that would be.

"I never told him that I knew. It was an accident that I even learned of his life in the city and the woman he loved. At least, I assume that was the case. They were together for a long time. Something happened about the time you were ten. He stopped spending so much time in the city, and I stopped things with Antonio. Silvano and I made a real effort at a relationship. That was when I had the miscarriage. I'd been so hopeful the baby was going to be a new beginning for us, but when I lost the pregnancy and became depressed, things slipped back to how they were. It was Antonio who helped bring me happiness again." Elena's voice is filled with love—the kind of love I always wanted for my father. He *is* a good man and deserves all the joy in the world.

"Another relationship?" His words are laced with pain.

"I'm sorry, I would prefer you not to think poorly of him, but if you're going to know the truth, you should know all of it."

"I agree. I'm just so stunned. He preached loyalty and honor every chance he had—having a mistress isn't *loyal*."

"That depends on your priorities. He was loyal to the family and what they expected of him. He tried to be loyal to his heart by not abandoning the woman he loved. And he was *always* loyal to you boys."

"Just not you." Z is quiet for several beats of my racing heart. "Well, I truly am happy to hear that Tony has been such a positive part of your life. I regret that I spent so many years hating him."

"That's the thing," Elena says warmly. "None of us are

perfect. We're all doing the best we can in the circumstances given."

Z pauses. "Do you know if Dad had other children with this woman?"

"I, ah ... I don't. I never pushed to learn about their life there." Her tone changes with a sort of wariness or ... guilt?

Zeno must also sense the shift. "I know about Nevio, Mom. You've no need to worry."

"You do?" she asks incredulously.

"Yes. I secretly ran tests to confirm my suspicions back when I first moved to the city. It doesn't change anything, at least as far as I'm concerned. I suppose that's why I decided to tell you what I know. Nevio's paternity doesn't change that he's my brother, and who you choose to love doesn't change my love for you."

"Oh, Z," she whispers.

From the sound of it, the two hug, and I have to wipe at tears pooling on my lashes. I'm so grateful they've finally been open with one another.

"I didn't handle things back then as I would now, and I'm sorry for that," Zeno offers quietly.

"No need for apologies," she assures him. "You know I'm so incredibly proud of you, and it fills my heart with joy to see you so happy with Luisa."

"I won't do what Dad did, you know." His voice is barely above a murmur, and I have to strain to hear him. "I'll devote my life to making her happy."

"I know you will, sweet boy. I see how much you love Isa. You two are already in such a better place than your father and I ever were."

I'm not sure my heart can stand much more love without bursting at the seams. I wipe at my eyes again to make sure there's no evidence of my eavesdropping and pray any redness can be attributed to waking up. After taking a deep breath, I walk around the corner in my best just-came-down-the-stairs impression.

"Hey!" I grin. "Am I interrupting?"

"Not at all," Elena beams. "Come have a seat."

I walk toward Zeno with the intent of sitting beside him, but he yanks me onto his lap. I squeal with surprise and peer at Elena, hoping our display of affection doesn't make her uncomfortable. The grin on her face is the antithesis of discomfort. She truly is ecstatic for us.

"Zeno and I have been having a heart-to-heart, but I suspect you already know everything we've discussed." Elena looks at Zeno questioningly.

I go stock-still, sure I've been busted for eavesdropping.

"Yes, I've already told Luisa everything," Z admits. "I hope it doesn't upset you that I shared something so personal."

*Oh, thank God. They don't know I was listening.*

My lips hitch in an awkward smile.

"No, not at all. You two shouldn't have secrets between you. I wouldn't want that for you." She looks at me and grins mischievously. "You gave me quite the scare when you first moved back in with your parents. I kept seeing you with Nevio and didn't know what to do about it—like the day you two were under the trees together."

"Under the trees together?" Zeno's voice takes on a predatory edge as his fingers dig playfully into my ribs.

I squirm with a giggle. "You mean the day the housekeeper broke the window?" It's the only time I can recall being under the trees with Nevio where Elena could have seen us.

"Yes!" She laughs. "Only because I was freaking out and told her to break it. I had to stop you two from doing something you'd regret. Then you moved up your date, and I didn't realize it. When I found out, I worried to death. I talked to your father, and he assured me nothing happened and that he'd take care of it." She pauses, growing serious. "I hope it doesn't upset you to hear me talk about him."

"Not at all. I'm glad he has you, actually. I don't know how I didn't see it before, but he cares deeply for you."

A radiant blush warms her cheeks, and her gentle smile speaks to her own love for him.

I squeeze Zeno's hand and continue. "Did he tell you he's divorcing Mom?"

Z shifts to catch my gaze. "He is? You didn't say anything."

"It's been a crazy couple of weeks." I shrug and turn back to Elena.

"He told me he was filing," she confirms.

"I heard them argue the other day when he first told Mom. She knew about you guys. She even knew about Nevio."

All the color drains from Elena's face. "I had no idea."

"It's not a huge deal. I suppose Dad told you that Mom was with someone else, too."

She nods. "Yes, I knew the girls weren't his. I'm just

surprised she wasn't bothered by my relationship with him."

"Honestly, you had something to offer her. She never cared enough about Dad to justify confronting you and possibly losing her place at Hardwick. I think she figured she could keep the information in her back pocket as leverage, but she didn't know about Dad's vasectomy. In a way, I guess their secrets canceled each other out."

"Well, at least we're all moving forward." Elena breathes a deep sigh, her shoulders sagging with relief.

I peer at Zeno and gnaw on my lip. "Yeah, no more secrets. Soooo, it's okay that I told Gia, right?"

Z's eyes widen ever so slightly in rebuke.

"I had to talk it through with *someone*. And Gia wouldn't tell a soul. However, that means Nevio and my younger sister are the only people in our families who don't know the truth. I can't help but wonder if Nevio should be told. I would never say anything myself, but it's bound to come out eventually, and personally, I think he deserves to know." I glance between mother and son with an apologetic expression. I want to speak my mind, but it's a sensitive subject, and I don't want to upset them.

Z looks to his mother and shrugs. "I suppose it's up to you."

Worry creases her forehead. "I don't want him to hate me, but maybe you're right. I'll have to think about it."

I give her a reassuring smile.

"Well, then," Z says, patting my leg. "I've got an appointment with my lawyer in a few hours. I need to get cleaned up and head to the city."

It's Sunday, which is an unusual day for meetings with lawyers, but his boss was murdered last night. I imagine that qualifies as an emergency.

Elena jumps up. "I'll cook some eggs. Sausage or bacon?"

"Bacon," Zeno and I say in unison.

I giggle and poke Z in the ribs—payback for his earlier tickles. He grunts and slaps my backside as I scurry after Elena.

# CHAPTER 18

One Month Later

"Hey, you two! What's with all the boxes?" Ari walks up to where Zeno and I are waiting for the lobby elevator at his city apartment. *Our* apartment. I've been staying with him for a couple of weeks, but we're only now officially moving all my stuff. It's strange to think of his place being mine too.

"It's moving day. Classes are starting soon, so I needed to get settled in the city." I haven't seen much of Ari in the last month. We've both been busy adjusting to major life changes. Now that Christiano is gone, Ari's life is her own, and freedom looks good on her. She was already beautiful, but now her hard edges have softened. She seems content in a way she didn't before. "What are you up to?"

"I've decided to sell Dad's apartment and am meeting with a real estate agent to start the process. I thought about renovating and keeping the place—it has phenomenal views, as you know—but I'd rather move on."

"That's understandable."

Ari's gaze lingers on Zeno. "How've you been, Z? Adjusting to your new position?"

His lips quirk upward fondly when he looks at her, and I get the sense that something passes between them.

"No complaints here." He glances at the elevator doors, which have opened and closed with other passengers while we've been chatting. "If you're looking to sell, though, I might be in the market."

I peer back at him, brows raised.

He shrugs. "The security's better on the top floor. More space. We could live in my place while we renovate the other—make it somewhere we're both at home."

I'm stunned, but what he says makes sense. And if memories of the prior owner won't bother him, then they won't bother me. I'd only been to the place once. "Okay." I look back at Ari with what must be a cartoonish smile.

She throws her head back and laughs from deep in her belly. "Okay, then. You give me a call, Z. We'll figure something out."

We take the elevator together, Z and I exiting on our floor while Ari continues upward.

"She seems like she's doing well," I say as we walk my stuff back to the guest bedroom, where we decided to stash things until I have time to go through them. "I'd say she's much happier without her father around."

Ari had been subjected to endless rounds of questioning about her father in the weeks after his shooting. From what Zeno tells me, no one has been able to pinpoint who took out the Giordano boss. The investigation isn't closed yet, but he doesn't think anything will come of it. If the family itself can't identify who instigated the attack, how could the cops have any hope of getting answers?

I've thought about that night a thousand times over and tried to reconstruct my memory. Like waking up from a dream and knowing the details will fade if I don't concentrate on preserving them. I feel an inexplicable need to remember.

"Did I ever mention that I had a long chat with the Guardian of the Gate about a week after Christiano was killed?" I follow Zeno into the living room, my eyes glued to his muscular back.

"Who?"

"You know, that new kid who works at the entry gate. I think his name is Adam, but after that first day when he wouldn't let me in, I dubbed him the Guardian of the Gate."

"I don't believe you mentioned that." He checks the stack of mail on the entry table, probably wondering where on earth I'm going with my story.

"He's not such a bad kid. Grew up in a small town in Jersey and did a couple of years in the Army."

Z cuts his eyes at me, brows raised impatiently.

I plop onto the sofa and open my phone. "It was funny. He made a joke about people always being in a hurry. Said he saw you flying past the front gates the night of the engagement dinner. I explained that it couldn't have been you because you were at the house with us, but he swore up and down that he'd seen you. Said he's learned the vehicles of all the residents." My eyes drift over and collide with his.

I hadn't mentioned the conversation I'd had for good reason. A sound part of me wondered if it might be true. Zeno had a substantial amount to gain from Christiano's death. And while I'd seen him pacing in his office, I haven't been able to shake the feeling that all of the events of that day were incredibly ... convenient.

Z prowls around the couch toward me. "I was at the house with you all evening. You saw me."

"I saw a man in your suit pacing in your office."

He lifts his chin and rubs his neck. "I suppose Savio and I could have changed suits. He could have pretended to be me, waiting in my office while I raced over to kill Christiano, but that would mean we were in on the plot together."

"Indeed, and I've struggled with finding ample motivation for him. Christiano was his uncle, after all. Why would Savio want him dead? Now, Ari, on the other hand. I've thought about Ari over and over. Thought about how demure she was around Christiano and how violent he was toward me—about those security cameras that were miraculously disabled. But what I've thought about the most is how upset she was when she saw her father dead and how grief could look strikingly similar to relief."

"That is an impressive scheme you've envisioned."

"It is rather imaginative, isn't it? No evidence left

behind for the authorities, a slew of witnesses could attest to the fact that you never left the estate, and who would think to question Ari's loyalty to her father? It only works if all three of you were in on it together, but if that was the case, it would nearly be the perfect crime."

"Except for you," he says quietly. "You questioned."

"Only because I had insights no one else would have."

Z leans in to prop himself over me using the back of the couch. Our faces inches apart, he drowns me in his turbulent gaze.

My heart skitters at his nearness, and my mind races with curiosity over what he'll say.

A minute passes before he lowers his mouth to my ear. "White wine or red?" he breathes seductively, effectively burying our conversation six feet under.

My own breath hitches before I can answer. "Red."

He slowly pulls away and strolls into the kitchen, and that's how I know we are meant for one another. Because Zeno De Rossi has killed for me, not once but twice, and it doesn't bother me in the slightest. He did what was necessary to keep me safe. I would do the same for him.

A love like ours is worth preserving at all costs, which is why this conversation will never happen again.

"What's for dinner?" I ask brightly, lifting from the sofa to join him in the kitchen.

He meets my gaze appreciatively. "Steak."

"Celebrating, are we?" I arch an eyebrow. It's our first official night living together, and it's sweet he's memorializing the occasion.

"Absolutely. You get the wine poured, and I'll start the food."

⁓

Two hours later, we take our wineglasses onto the balcony with full tummies and tired feet after a full day on the go. Z sits on the lounge chair with his legs on either side to make room for me in the middle. I lie back against his chest and hum approvingly when his arms wrap around me.

"It's a beautiful night," he murmurs.

"It is, and dinner was excellent. Thank you." I sip from my wine before he takes the glass and sets it on the table beside us to hold my hands in his. The wind blows steadily up between the buildings, giving us a perfect breeze as we admire the city below. I take in the splashes of neon color but am easily distracted by the sight of Zeno's hands touching mine. Holding and caressing.

"I never imagined I could be this happy," he says softly. His warm breath drifts past my ear. "Or that one person could change my life so completely."

"For some people, change is a dirty word."

"Well, in this case, change was a *very* good thing. You brought light to my world, Isa, and I want you with me always." His right hand lifts from beside us and produces a sparkling diamond ring between his fingers.

My lungs cease functioning. I can't breathe or think through the rush of emotion. All I can do is watch in bewildered awe as Zeno takes my now trembling left hand and slowly slides the ring onto my finger.

"Luisa Banetti, you are the most authentic, loyal, and passionate woman I've ever known. You live life on your terms, and I admire every single thing about you. I want nothing more in this world than for you to be my wife." He closes my fingers around his and brings my hand to his lips for a kiss. "Will you marry me, Isa?"

My watery gaze drifts from our hands back to his face as I twist in the chair toward him. Placing my ring-clad fingers on his cheek, I bring my lips to his. "Yes, Zeno. Forever and always, *yes*."

# EPILOGUE

5 Months Later

"Two girls—identical, no less. They're going to have their hands full." I lean against Zeno's side as we watch Livia open her next shower gift. We decided to throw one giant shower at Hardwick rather than coordinate several smaller gatherings among different groups of friends and family. After weeks of planning, the event is finally here and unfolding seamlessly.

Liv is seven months along and enormous. They learned at their first doctor visit that the couple was expecting twins. Identical girls, as they were told at a later ultrasound. It's a good thing they have money to hire help because I can't imagine Liv taking care of one baby, let alone two. She's fussed endlessly about how the girls are messing up her body, but I know she adores the attention she receives from a twin pregnancy.

"We'll need to keep a close eye on Nevio. The stress won't be easy on him," Z murmurs close to my ear.

"Yeah. At least he's done well leading up to this."

The couple's wedding was small, but Liv made sure to indulge in opulent selections at every opportunity—insisting on peonies because simple roses are too basic and rush ordering a dress from the most exclusive bridal boutique in the city. I don't want to know what the event cost. I don't even care. All that mattered was that Nevio played his part graciously, and Livia was deliriously happy.

I try not to think of how much they remind me of my parents.

Elena did decide to tell Nevio about his parentage and the affair. We were all worried about how he'd take the news, but it went surprisingly well. In fact, I think it gave him the justification he needed to reconcile who he is and why he has always been so different from the other men in his family. It also eased the sting of my rejection and gave us another avenue for connection. Between that news and a strict schedule with his therapist, Nevio seems to be finding contentment in life. He and Zeno have even started to spend time together in small intervals.

Liv and Nevio may remind me of my parents, but their story is unwritten and open to a world of possibilities.

Ripping through tissue paper, Livia pulls out a matching set of leopard-print bows from a shiny gift sack and swoons. "Oh ... my ... *God*! These are the cutest!"

Nevio raises his brows and shakes his head, making me laugh.

"Isa"—Gia snags my attention from behind—"would you mind terribly if I went on home? I'm not doing so well." Her face is positively green.

"Of course not. Go home and get some rest!" I squeeze her hand and smile at Carter, who hovers behind her with worry on his face.

The two are rarely apart, especially after they announced their own pregnancy a month earlier. Ever since, Gia has struggled with horrible morning sickness. It hasn't allowed much of a honeymoon period after their wedding. They exchanged vows in the most lovely, touching backyard ceremony I've ever been to. Boston stood by his father as best man, and Emily was a bridesmaid. Both children were utterly smitten with their new stepmom. And now, the family is over the moon with anticipation of its newest member.

Carter's sister, Cora, has kept her distance, much to everyone's delight. She showed up for the wedding but went back to the city first thing the next morning.

It's been an eventful six months since I first returned home for what was supposed to be a short visit. While the early days were turbulent, the seas have been calm and skies clear ever since Christiano's death. The investigation into his death has been closed without any further leads. With the backing of Savio and a majority of the other capos, Zeno took the helm as boss of the Giordano family. And as they'd planned when they were younger, Savio is now Z's consigliere. The two are inseparable. Savio even purchased Zeno's old apartment, but the renovations of our new place are still underway, so we aren't moving until they are complete. He still has no desire to live at Tuxedo Park, but that hasn't been an issue since we spend most of our time in the city.

I'm almost done with school and have even managed to write half of my book when I wasn't studying or planning weddings and showers. Besides Livia and Gia, I've had a wedding of my own to plan, though Zeno and I decided on a private destination ceremony for ourselves. We leave for Aruba the day after Christmas, a mere two weeks away. No one is going with us. They wanted to, and several people argued heartily that they shouldn't be denied access to our big day, but we weren't interested in pleasing others. Our wedding will be a day only for us. Heartfelt vows spoken to one another on the shores of paradise with no stress or expectations. Just Zeno and I together.

When we return, we'll host a world-class reception at a luxury hotel in the city where we can celebrate with all our friends and family. The arrangements have been made. My gown is ready, and my heart is full.

"Earth to Luisa." The hum of Zeno's masculine voice draws me from my thoughts.

"What?"

"The presents are about done. What comes next?"

"Oh, we'll thank everyone for coming and let them know they can stay as long as they like."

"That shouldn't be too long. Forecasters have upped the chances of snow for this evening."

I peer outside to the overcast skies. "That would be

amazing. I'd love to see a little snow before we head to the beach."

Z wraps his arm around my back. "Amazing for you, but Ari and Grace and several others will need to get back to the city before the roads get bad."

My eyes drift to my childhood friend who stands along the wall with her girlfriend, the two gently leaning into one another. After adjusting to the reality of her father's death, Ari began to flourish in her new life. She took over the management of one of her father's restaurants, and she and Grace became an official couple. Without Christiano around, the Mafia couldn't care less about her sexual preferences. As for the Larsons, though, they have struggled with understanding their daughter's relationship. They love her enormously, but they still refer to Ari as Grace's friend rather than partner or girlfriend. Hopefully, they'll come around with time.

I'm delighted for them. Grace is happier than ever and is working full-time for a theater company. She's kept her apartment, but the two spend almost all their time at Ari's place. I wouldn't be surprised if that arrangement becomes more permanent when Grace's lease is up.

The situation with my parents has been a little touch and go. Elena offered to help find Mom a new job at another house in the area, but I knew that wouldn't go over well. Mom has been convinced she won the son-in-law lottery and never has to work again. I've been reluctant to enable such entitlement, yet I can't seem to justify turning her away when we *do* have so much wealth. She is my mother, after all.

Zeno and I came to an agreement with Gia and Carter to jointly provide a fixed monthly stipend for Mom under the strict stipulation that no other allotments will be made. If she gets herself in trouble with her spending or gambling, that will be her problem. We are providing her more than she probably deserves.

She moved into an apartment a few weeks ago and has given Dad minimal recoil over the divorce. He's stayed at the cottage and can often be found at Hardwick, but he and Elena haven't openly proclaimed a relationship. Maybe they never will. I can't say what will happen, but both are happier than they've been in a long time, and that's enough for me.

With Livia and Mom out of the cottage, Dad gave Marca the choice of taking over Gia's job at Hardwick or going to school for her associate's degree. Much to my delight, she chose school and has become surprisingly engrossed in her studies.

"I suppose I'll start cleaning up," I tell Z.

Livia is on her feet, giving a tearful thanks to her guests. A double dose of hormones has wreaked havoc on her already volatile emotions. Fortunately, Nevio's laid-back personality has kept him seemingly unfazed. He hands her a tissue, and the two begin saying goodbye to their parting guests.

An hour later, all that remains in the house are those of us here for the night. Nevio helps Liv waddle upstairs to rest, and Elena disappears along with my father. The two housekeepers scurry about, collecting dishes and discarded wrapping paper. Wanting to help, I gather several punch glasses near our seats to take to the kitchen. I set them on the counter and pause before leaving when I spot an extra stack of printed "Oh Baby" napkins left out on the table. I pick one up and run my fingers over the custom floral design around the edges. They matched perfectly with the floral arrangements and other décor. I was extremely happy with how well it all turned out.

"Sorry about that," Zeno says as he joins me at the table. He'd had to take a call while we were sending off the last of the guests.

"No problem." I smile at him and peer back down at the napkin.

"Something wrong?"

"No, I was just debating whether to throw these away or keep them." My heart begins a frantic dance in my chest.

"Keep them?" he asks, confused.

"I've debated all day how to tell you—" I peer into those aqua eyes I adore so deeply as tears burn in my own. "I wasn't sure until this morning, but it looks like we'll be needing a shower of our own come summer."

Zeno is momentarily motionless, his lips slightly parted. "You're pregnant?" he breathes.

I nod, desperately hoping his casual attitude about children wasn't simply a show because I hadn't meant for this to happen so quickly. We'd discussed me getting off birth control, but who would have thought I'd be pregnant the very first month? Not me.

Banishing my fears, Zeno displays a triumphant grin as he yanks me into his arms and spins me around. I squeal and laugh, clutching him tightly. When he slows our dizzying circles, my feet touch back down, and our gazes lock in a silent communication of ardent love.

"I didn't think you could make me any happier than I already was. But as you are so good at doing, you've proven me wrong. I love you *so fucking much*." His lips melt into mine, a sensual glide imparting every ounce of his passion and devotion.

Our journey to this place in time may have been arduous, but now that we're here, I can unequivocally say the struggle was worth the reward. I love Zeno De Rossi with all my soul and will continue to do so until the end of time.

*The End*<br>
Sort of…<br>
Keep reading for four bonus chapters told from Zeno's point of view!

# CHAPTER 1

WHAT THE HELL IS TAKING SO LONG? A GATED COMMUNITY sounds good in theory, but the time I spend waiting to get in and out of this place is ridiculous. I've just spent ten minutes behind some piece of shit Ford Focus while the driver tries to argue his way past the guard. Normally, I'm a patient man—especially compared to some of my associates—but it's been a shit week. Planning a funeral while processing the loss of my father has made me more than a little short-tempered.

Scathing words perched on my tongue, I reach for the door handle when the passenger of the car ahead of me storms into view. She can't see past my tinted windows, but I can see her perfectly.

Luisa Banetti—a name I whisper in my dreams where no one else can hear. The girl I grew up with, and the woman I've spent a decade trying to protect. Always from a distance. Never allowing myself to get too close.

The sight of her douses my anger with a bucket of icy cold water. I'm propelled from the car but for entirely different reasons—a gravitational pull beyond my control. I need to see her without a layer of bulletproof glass between us.

"Do we have a problem here?" I could wring the guard's scrawny neck for giving her trouble.

Luisa blanches at my tone, no doubt believing my irritation is directed at her. It's a logical assumption, considering our past and the way I've behaved toward her. I desperately want to correct her—to explain how my feelings for her have changed over the years—but our history feels like an insurmountable mountain to climb.

"Hello, Z." Her voice is a melody that soothes the darkest parts of my soul. A siren song that tempts and shames me because I want what I cannot have. What I have stricken from the realm of possibilities.

"Luisa." I put more force behind the word than I should in an attempt to rein in my emotions. I must keep my distance.

The guard says something, but his words only buzz at my ears like the annoying hum of a mosquito. I have my attention securely fixed on Luisa.

"I wasn't informed you were coming." A fact, but in light of the strain between us, the statement is an affront. An unintentional rebuff. I hate that the energy between us coats everything we say with a residue of oily distaste.

Luisa's spine stiffens. "I wasn't aware my family had to inform you of my visits."

*They don't. I only meant to express my surprise. I'm pleased you're here.*

Except I can't say any of those things. I can't do anything to encourage her to come near Hardwick when my brother might be coming to stay.

*Our* brother.

After avoiding disaster for over a decade, I won't see all that effort wasted in a moment of weakness.

"Considering the circumstances, the information would have been appreciated." Instead, I pass off my statement as part of the planning process for Dad's funeral. Surely, that's why she's here. She'll understand my need to estimate the number of guests at the wake and funeral luncheon. It's what I should be concerned about—not some idealized fantasy of a woman who hates me. I have to contain my rioting emotions and not lose track of reality. My father has died, and now it's even more important that I protect his honor and take care of my family. I turn my attention to the guard. "Luisa is a member of the estate. You can put her on the list of universally approved."

I walk away without another word. Saying anything more to Luisa will only lead to frustration and pain. It's best if we keep to our designated lanes and maintain the status quo. She can continue to believe I'm a cold, ruthless monster so long as I know she's safe and happy. So long as Nevio stays far away from her, and our family secrets remain in the dark.

# CHAPTER 2

"Yeah?" Savio answers his phone with an unusual degree of exasperation. I'm instantly on alert. He's too easygoing for me to overlook a change in his countenance.

"You have a problem with me calling?" I ask, distracted from my original reason for calling.

"Not at all. I just got instructions from De Bellis to join him for dinner tonight, and I am not in the fucking mood."

Sav has always hated his uncle. He hasn't told me the specifics, but Savio used to spend a month in the summers with Christiano and his daughter, Ari. I don't know what went on during those visits, but Christiano De Bellis is the one man who can rile up Savio in ten seconds flat.

"With the way he's kissing your ass lately, it won't be an issue. Listen, I finished up early with Wagner. Everything is in order for the next few months."

"That's great. You have to schmooze with his wife this time?"

"No, thank fuck." The mayor of New York City is a sleazy motherfucker, but it's his wife I have to look out for. I've never met such a handsy sixty-five-year-old woman. "Listen, I need to crash at your place for the next couple of nights."

"What the hell is wrong with your place?"

I breathe deeply, trying not to imagine Luisa in my apartment because I like the idea too goddamn much. "I've got company."

"You let someone stay at your place? While you're not there?" His voice pitches high with his incredulity.

I hadn't thought this through. Now, I'm going to have to explain. Should have just gone to a fucking hotel. "Just a family friend," I say with an intentional degree of detachment. "The Banettis help run Hardwick, and one of their daughters is here for a couple of nights. I was being polite."

What a joke. Politeness had nothing to do with it. I'd jumped at the chance to offer up my home the second Antonio Banetti had mentioned Luisa was spending the weekend in the city. Christ knows I owe the woman, but that wasn't all of it. I wanted her in my space. Touching my things and leaving traces of herself where I might find them. I'd had some seriously stalkerish thoughts but had no desire to explain that to Savio—friend or no friend.

"This is starting to make sense," he says. "You're talking about Luisa Banetti, right?"

Every muscle in my body instantly goes rigid. "Yeah, why?"

"I couldn't remember where I knew the name, but De Bellis mentioned her when he invited me for dinner tonight. Guess he's invited her as well."

*Jesus Christ!* Luisa's going to be at Christiano's? *Fuck.* There is no fucking way I'm letting that happen unless I'm there to watch over her.

"Looks like I'm crashing your dinner."

Savio is silent on the other end, but I can envision the smile creeping across his smug face. "Family friend, huh?" he finally jabs.

"Shut up, asshole. I'll be at your place in an hour. Wait for me." I hang up and clench the steering wheel with renewed force, suddenly pissed that there's too much goddamn traffic.

I HAVE to remind myself to breathe when I lay eyes on Luisa a little over an hour later. I'd wanted to go straight to Christiano's place so she wouldn't end up alone with him, but my unexpected appearance would have been harder to explain. If I arrived with Savio, I could shrug off crashing dinner as a natural consequence of staying with him. That meant we couldn't show up early, so Isa and her friend were already in the lion's den when we arrived.

Luisa is breathtaking on a normal day. Tonight, she is otherworldly. Her gray dress hugs her every curve, creating ripples of fabric that I want to explore like a road map of her body. The near black eye shadow she's wearing accentuates the most incredible blue eyes I've ever seen.

My own eyes are blue, but hers have a ring of gold in the center like a circle of flame—ice and fire melded together. Her irises are as multidimensional as she is, and I struggle not to lose myself in their depths.

I have to actively convince my dick not to salute her because she's so goddamn enchanting.

"Savio, I see you brought a guest." Christiano's grating voice fills the room, effectively reining in my desire. This man is too conniving not to be on guard in his presence.

"I was telling Z that I had plans to join you for dinner, and he said he'd wrapped up his business early, so I invited him to join us. I hope that's not a problem." Ever the loyal friend, Savio does a masterful job of passing off my presence.

"Of course not," Christiano says stiffly.

I don't believe him for a second. I'm not sure why he'd prefer my absence, but it assures me I did the right thing by coming. Whatever his reasons, I am unlikely to approve. He continues with introductions and focuses the ensuing discussion on Luisa. I'm so on edge worrying about Christiano's motivations that I'm terse when the conversation comes around to me. I can sense Luisa's discomfort. Her general anxiety about dining with my boss is multiplied by her concern that I'll interpret her presence as an intrusion. I want to assure her otherwise, but I have to do my best to appear unaffected. Any sign that I have an interest in her won't be overlooked by my vigilant Giordano boss. I don't want to give him any more reason than he already has to remember the name Luisa Banetti.

I spend the entire evening fighting the constant pull to

gravitate into her orbit. I don't look in her direction, I pretend to be distracted when she is the focus of our conversation, and I certainly don't leave until she is safely away from Christiano.

By the time the night is over, I'm equal parts relief and frustration. While I successfully neutralized the De Bellis threat, I also came off acting like a dick. It seems no matter how I feel about Luisa, I'm put in a position to drive her away from me.

The drive to Savio's place is made in near silence. He is absorbed in his own thoughts while I obsess over what Luisa might be thinking or doing. After the way I acted, I wouldn't blame her if she went straight to my bathroom and swirled my toothbrush in the toilet. I deserve that and so much worse after the years of torment I've dished out.

When I'm finally in the privacy of Savio's guest room, I give in to my agonizing curiosity. Booting up my laptop, I log in remotely to my security feed. When I first offered the use of my apartment, I told myself I wouldn't intrude on her privacy in this manner. I knew I'd be tempted and specifically warned myself not to violate her trust. She may think I'm a horrible human being, but I don't have to live up to her doctored view of me.

However, my willpower proves pathetic compared to my crippling obsession.

I tell myself that I might as well earn the reputation I've created. My rationale doesn't matter. The truth is, I'll tell myself whatever I need to hear to give myself permission to pull up those cameras and get her on screen.

Live feed of the apartment reveals that the girls have

shut down for the night. Luckily, my system is designed to record at night as well as during the day. I keep the bedroom cameras off when I'm home and am confident enough in my setup not to worry about hackers or leaked footage. Security is crucial for someone in my line of work.

I rewind the digital recording by an hour to when Luisa and Grace first returned to the apartment after dinner. They have a short conversation before retreating to the two guest bedrooms. I wish I knew what they were saying, but the system doesn't record sound. I fast-forward and switch to the guest bedroom camera to follow Isa. I can't see her when she's in the bathroom, but I watch her settle into bed and turn out the lights. I stare longer than I should at her motionless form. There's only so much leniency I can give myself before I have to admit I'm pushing the limits on being certifiably obsessed. However, before I can click to log out of the system, she throws back the covers and slips from her room.

I'm instantly on alert.

I trace her movements through the house from one camera to the next. When she starts in the direction of my room, my lungs seize.

*What is she doing? Why is she sneaking into my bedroom under the cover of darkness?*

I would give everything I'm worth to know what she's thinking at this moment, but that's a secret not even money can buy. All I can do is watch intently as she tiptoes into my room.

The second she climbs onto my bed, my dick surges to life.

Watching her is the most exquisite torture I've ever experienced. Her hand grazes over the expensive cotton fabric of my comforter, and I feel her phantom touch caress my skin. It's too much. I have to clutch my dick through my pants to ease the ache. When she lies back on the pillows, and her hand goes to her breast, I nearly come.

*Jesus* fucking *Christ. She's going to be the death of me.*

How, after all the horrible things I've said and done to her, could she possibly see me as anything but a monster? I'd been hesitant to believe myself when I thought I detected a tendril of desire from her in the past weeks. I had told myself it was wishful thinking—that she couldn't possibly want me—but as I watch with disbelieving eyes as her knees spread wide and her hand disappears beneath her panties, I know I wasn't wrong. Some part of her, no matter how small and deviant, is drawn to me.

It's all I need for hope to take root.

Hope that the situation I've created isn't totally irreversible.

Without taking my eyes from the screen, I undo my pants and fist my cock. It swells angrily with need, making my head spin as all my blood drains south. I begin to work myself, hand pumping greedily up and down my dick. It feels so fucking good. Better than simply rubbing one out because she's there, writhing in my bed, teasing me to a point of madness. My balls pull so tight, I wonder if they might spontaneously combust. I could be the first man on earth to lose a testicle from explosive lust.

She'd be one-hundred-percent worth it.

I'm so lost in my own desire that she catches me by

surprise when she thrusts her face into my pillow and spasms with her release. The sight instantly triggers my own undoing. And like some inexperienced teenage boy with no clue what's going on, I come all over the fucking place.

I don't give a single fuck.

Witnessing what I did—confirming Isa could be mine—is worth cleaning up a fucking truckload of cum. Hearing the recorded moans she'd accidentally texted me had been hot, but this? Thoughts of this will get me through months of lonely nights.

Slowly, my breathing begins to regulate. I refocus on the video when she jumps from the bed, seemingly panicked. It only takes a minute to realize what's going on.

I'm not the only one who's made a mess.

I can see a dark smudge on the comforter when she races to the bathroom. Isa clearly has no problem getting wet. If the video feed were live, I could text her and assure her that I don't give a damn about the bedding. Quite the opposite. I'm fucking ecstatic to see the evidence of her desire for me. But the scene I'm witnessing is just an echo of what's already happened. Reaching out to her now would only be awkward.

Tomorrow, I'll find a reason to see my girl. And that's what she is—my girl. She just doesn't know it yet. I'll have to prove to her I'm worthy of her trust and, if at all possible, make up for what I've done. I'm not sure how, and it won't be easy, but I don't care. Luisa Banetti *will* be mine.

# CHAPTER 3

WHAT A WASTE OF MY TIME. I SPENT AN ENTIRE DAY pretending to enjoy myself at some dickhead's Hamptons estate when all I wanted to do was get back to Hardwick and Luisa. We swam and grilled and did jack shit that required my presence, but Christiano had insisted I join him. Now, I'm in one of the old guy's many guest rooms shutting down for the night, wishing there was a lock on my door. I don't like staying at other people's places if I don't call them a friend. But again, Christiano insisted.

I lie back in the ostentatious bed—solid wood with intricate carvings so busy they give me a headache—and open my phone to check the emails I've been forced to ignore all day. I only make it through the first of a long list when a call from my mother appears on the screen. It's almost eleven. She's rarely awake at this time, let alone calling me.

"Mom, what's happened?"

"Z, I'm so sorry to bother you." Her voice is hushed but frantic, spurring me to my feet.

"Are you in danger?" I can have men at the house in minutes if needed.

"No—at least, I don't think so. It's Isa."

My blood hardens into ice. Every muscle in my body coils in preparation of what she'll say next.

"She showed up at the house with a knife covered in blood. She was terrified—said she may have killed a man. I think someone broke into their home. I have her in the shower now, and the knife is wrapped in a towel downstairs, but I don't know what else to do."

*What in the ever-loving fuck?*

Tuxedo Park is safe. That's why I don't normally worry about Mom there alone. Who the fuck would dare to attack someone on my estate? And of all people, whoever this man is, he chose the wrong damn woman to go after. If he isn't dead already, he's going to wish he had died when I get my hands on him.

"Don't say another word. I'm leaving now." I hang up and am in my car in record time. I don't even tell anyone I'm leaving.

It's a small miracle I make it to Hardwick without a ticket. I've never experienced three more agonizing hours —racking my brain over what could have happened and wondering if Isa is hurt. I'm desperate to get to her.

When I finally get to the house, Mom is still up, waiting

for me. I reassure her that I'll handle everything and send her to bed, then take the stairs two at a time. The bedroom door is closed, but dim light peeks out from beneath. I silently let myself in. The bathroom light casts a soft glow into the room, revealing Isa curled into a ball in the center of the bed.

Savage emotions clamp down on my chest, constricting my breathing.

She looks so tiny. So innocent. It's my job to protect her, and I failed. I hadn't even known she was in any danger. My degree of shame is only matched by a towering inferno of rage. I would give in to the bloodlust this instant and hunt down the man responsible, but I need to hear from her what happened first. I need information, no matter how much I hate forcing her to relive the experience.

Sitting in an armchair by the bed, I hesitate to disturb her sleep. Her moment of peace. God knows when she wakes, she'll be haunted by the memories. Mom told me Isa had been covered in blood. Something like that takes a toll on someone so sensitive. So pure and kind.

I would give anything to erase this stain from her memories.

But that's not possible. The best I can do is ensure she's never put in this position again. That she always feels safe and secure. And she will, so long as I'm breathing.

A few short minutes later, Luisa rockets upright. Her frantic gaze collides with mine as though she sensed my presence. Sensed she wasn't alone. Her fear is palpable, and it turns my heart to cinders.

"It's okay, Isa. It's just me," I reassure her.

"Z." The relief encapsulated in the single syllable is overwhelming. Never in all my life have I been received with such desperate urgency.

I'm on my way to her in an instant—no thought to our past or what might be right or wrong in the situation. I move on instinct alone. She must do the same because all pretenses are gone. When I sit on the bed, she climbs into my lap, and I welcome her. The feel of her soft, feminine form is exactly the reassurance I need. My Isa is okay. Traumatized but alive.

"Jesus, you had me worried. I've never driven so fast in my life." I breathe in the clean scent of her hair, still wet from her shower.

"I'd say I'm sorry to pull you away from work, but I'm not," she whispers.

Even if I had been doing something important, it would be meaningless without her. I don't want her to ever question my dedication.

I pull back and meet her troubled gaze, intending to assure her that she is my top priority when the sight of her battered cheek comes into view. Words escape me. Isa defended herself, but not before this man laid hands on her. What else did he do to her?

*Jesus fuck.*

My hand finds her face, touching the edge of the injury I should have prevented. What other harm did he cause before she escaped? If he hurt her sexually, I'll burn down the entire motherfucking country to find him. I'll rip out his spleen and make him eat that shit, all while I watch without an ounce of remorse.

No one—fucking *no one*—hurts what's mine.

I take a slow breath to steady my voice. "I need you to tell me every way he hurt you."

Her eyes widen a fraction with understanding. "He didn't touch me like that. He wanted to, but I got away before he could."

*Thank Christ.*

If he'd touched her like that, I wouldn't be able to think past my fury. At least this way, I can maintain a modicum of control. While I mentally step back from the cliff's edge, Isa shifts in my lap to face me. She straddles me in a way that makes my dick as hard as concrete. He's insisting her movement is suggestive, but that can't be the case. How could she possibly want me after everything she's just gone through?

Even if she does, it's wrong of me to take advantage of her when she's vulnerable.

I try to fight off the urges, but when her lips hesitantly find mine, I'm swept away in the moment. I surrender to the need that crackles between us, a guttural moan of defeat clawing from deep in my throat.

"Fuck, I don't deserve this." Not on any level.

"No talking about the past," she says urgently. "We can deal with it later. Right now, we need this. *I* need this."

That's all she has to say to erase the last of my reservations.

I worship her body with the fervor I've only ever been able to exhibit in my darkest fantasies. Moments of weakness when I let myself imagine what it would be like if there were no secrets between us. What it would be like if I could show her exactly how I feel about her. I channel all of that pent-up desire and allow my devotion to rain down upon her.

The taste of her on my tongue is incredible—better than I ever imagined—but it's the feel of my cock sank deep inside her that changes me. As though our connection somehow alters my DNA, I feel my world shift beneath me. I am no longer a man seeking to survive on this earth—success and survival aren't my purpose. Every breath I take from this moment on will be in pursuit of Luisa. Claiming her, protecting her, providing for her—she has become my reason for being.

From the best part of my world to the only part that matters.

And that is why I lay with her until she drifts asleep, giving in to her demand to stay with her, but only so long as she is awake. I want her to feel safe, but I won't be able to rest until I eliminate all threats against her. Once I'm sure she's succumbed to her dreams, I quietly slip away.

I walk to the cottage in the dark, not wanting to drive and give away my arrival should her attacker still be there waiting for her return. Aldo Consoli. A fucking leach of a man, and the son of one of Christiano's longtime friends. Coincidence? Not fucking likely.

The lights are still on inside, giving me a perfect view through the windows. The place looks normal, aside from music blaring from the living room speakers at four in the morning. Gun in hand, I open the back door and scan the kitchen. A trail of blood winds from the door to the other side of the small island. Not a ton, but too much to be drips from the knife when Isa fled. My guess is that Aldo exited the back door, but whether to follow her or to seek help, I don't know.

I cautiously search the rest of the house and find it empty. There is no other sign of the injured man inside or out. He left alive, and the discovery brings me a surprising degree of relief—it's hard to punish a dead man.

Time to start the hunt.

I place two calls before beginning to clean up the blood splatter. First, I call in two soldiers to start twenty-four-hour protection duty. Second, I reach out to Savio and enlist his help with the search. We'll have to be careful because our actions could get back to Christiano and instigate a civil war. Technically, I'd need his blessing to kill another member of our organization. Especially if that man was acting under the boss's orders. I'd rather not have to conduct a coup, but I'm not afraid of it either. Aldo will die, and if that brings down the boss's wrath, then so be it.

LESS THAN TWENTY-FOUR HOURS LATER, I'm walking into a vacant warehouse to confront a dead man. He's not dead yet, but he will be soon enough. He was too stupid to exist anyway. As if going after Luisa wasn't proof enough of his ineptitude, he went to one of our family doctors to get stitched up, then back to his shit apartment to recover. He didn't even try to hide.

I'm almost disappointed that it was so easy.

"Aldo Consoli, what a pleasure." I stroll toward the center of the open room where Aldo is tied to a chair. He doesn't look so great—pale with a broken nose and a black eye to match Luisa's. Judging by the coloring, I'd say it happened before my men brought him in. "Don't tell me you let a girl beat the shit out of you?" I goad him only because I know a worthless creep like him will be mortified at being bested by a woman. I'm not so narrow-minded to think a man weak for losing a fight to a woman solely because of her gender. I know of at least one made woman who could probably castrate me if she wanted to. But to Aldo, this is an unspeakable insult, and I plan to injure him in every way I can.

He spits on the floor in my direction. "Only because I'd had a few drinks."

"Must have been more than a few. That or ... you're shit at handling your booze."

Savio chuckles from behind me, where he leans against the wall to watch the spectacle. He and I have been a team for too long for this to unfold without him, but he's not the type to get his hands dirty. Not in the literal sense. Anymore, I rarely do my own heavy lifting either, but this is different. Personal.

"Nothin' to do with me. That bitch went fuckin' kamikaze on me."

My eye twitches at his unkind reference to Luisa. "I think, perhaps, you simply lack the proper empathy to appreciate her perspective." My voice softens with an eerily threatening calm.

Aldo must hear the subtly camouflaged threat because his eyes dart around the room. "Hey, man. You can't do this. I was there on orders."

"I'm glad you brought that up. I'd love to hear all about those orders. Last I checked, we don't instruct our soldiers to assault women." I look at Savio in question. "Sav? Isn't that your understanding?"

"Right there with you."

We both look back at Aldo, who now has a sheen of sweat glistening on his forehead.

"Look, none of this is my fault. I was doing my job, collecting a family debt. That was the first time I ever laid eyes on her. Then the only reason I saw her again was because I'd been ordered to watch her—see what was going on between you two. I had every right to be there. She's the one who escalated things. Acting all flirty and inviting me in. Just like a bitch to lead a guy on, then cry rape." By the time he's done, ranting about his deluded fantasies, I'm clenching my fists so tight my knuckles are screaming. Partially to keep me from ripping his fucking head off but also because he's confirmed what I'd already suspected. Christiano let his ridiculous scheming go too far. He'd known something was up from the minute he saw Luisa in my apartment and had purposely set this creatin on her.

Being with me had made her a target.

I look over at Savio, whose troubled gaze is already fixed on me. He's come to the same conclusion. We've discussed what to do about Christiano's ruthless ambitions but haven't had cause to act. This turn of events changes that, and we both know it. We can't allow this sort of thing to destroy our organization.

I turn back to Aldo, forcing myself to focus on one problem at a time. "Unfortunately, Aldo, you've proven my point. Perspective isn't your strong suit. But no worries, we're about to expand your horizons." I place my fingers between my lips and whistle sharply. Seconds later, a trusted soldier wheels in a table outfitted with handcuffs. Normally, this can be used for lashes or other forms of punishment, but tonight, it will be used to teach a different sort of lesson.

I walk to another table in the back of the room and examine the tools laid out. They might be of use later, but for now, I need something different. "Sav, did you see any beer bottles in the office by chance?"

"Might be some in the trash. I can check." He strolls toward the front of the building.

Aldo's eyes are now millimeters from popping loose of their sockets. "What the fuck, man? What are you gonna do?"

"I think it's time you knew what it felt like to fear for the sanctity of your body. To know what a woman goes through when a man threatens to violate her ... and to lose that fight. Then perhaps, you can leave this earth repentant for what you've done."

The smell of ammonia fills the air when Aldo pisses himself.

Sometimes, I wonder if my life might be better on the right side of the law. More downtime and less demanding problems. But at moments like this, I'm forever grateful that I am not limited to the impotence of law enforcement and the judicial system as my sole source of recourse. I happily choose the danger of a life outside the law. It's not for everyone, but it's the only life I've ever known, and I wouldn't trade it for the world.

"Gentlemen, get him on the table. Facedown."

I go to sleep that night comforted by the memory of Aldo's final screams, reassured that he'll never go near Luisa again. The immediate threat is over, but we can no longer sit by and watch Christiano meddle in our lives. He has to be stopped, one way or another.

# CHAPTER 4

SAVIO'S STEELY GAZE BORES INTO ME AS HE POURS ME A whiskey. I haven't told him why I've called this impromptu meeting, but he knew my intent the second Arianna De Bellis showed up. The three of us would need to meet secretly at his apartment for only one reason. He and I have discussed the problems surrounding Christiano's role in leadership, but this is the first time we're bringing Ari into the fold. Savio has assured me in the past that she can be trusted. I've been hesitant to take the risk of sharing our concerns with her and am only doing it now because I've been given no other choice.

We must take action against Christiano.

"You two going to tell me what the hell is going on here?" Ari's eyes cut from me to Savio, sharp with keen intelligence. She knows this is no social call.

"Don't look at me." Savio raises his brows and lifts his hands. "This is all Z."

I glower at him. "I may not have submitted an agenda for our little meeting, but you know goddamn well what this is about. It's not the first time we've discussed the issue." I turn my gaze back to Ari and try to calm my temper. "We're taking a risk here by bringing you into the loop, but Savio assures me you're trustworthy."

The two of them exchange a glance rife with understanding. Their childhood years together bonded them more than most cousins. They bore a common tormentor.

"Things have gotten bad, Ari," I begin to explain. "Your father's delusions about our expected marriage have caused him to harm an innocent woman. He's not going to relinquish the fantasy, and I'm concerned about what he might do next. Suppose he discovers your ... preferences. What if you start seeing someone regularly? Would that person be in danger as well?" I stare at her pointedly, letting her imagine the possibilities.

Ari's tongue wets her lips. "Are you talking about Luisa? Did he hurt her?"

"I am. He sent a scumbag bookie around her place under the pretense of keeping an eye on her neighbor Grace. The bookie has a habit of getting drunk and deciding consent is overrated. It's an issue we should have put an end to long ago. I have no doubt your father was well aware of the situation he created."

The blood drains from her face. "Grace?" she whispers.

Savio and I exchange a glance. I'd been at the dinner

when she and Grace met, but judging by her reaction, I'd say Grace means more to her than I realized.

"Yes. It turns out this bookie loaned her money." I see the panic well in her eyes and raise a hand to calm her. "The debt nor the bookie are an issue anymore. Both have been taken care of, but that still leaves us with one problem."

Relief softens her posture though her gaze is sharper than ever when she meets my eyes. "What exactly do you propose?" Her words are calm but wary. She's afraid, but she knows as well as we do that Christiano will ruin us if we don't stop him. Seeing her accept that truth is an enormous relief. Having Ari on our side will make everything easier.

"There is no concrete plan yet. That's what we need to discuss."

"Is there any way to do this that doesn't end in his death?"

Savio takes the opportunity to chime in. "The chances are slim, but we won't rule out anything until all angles have been assessed."

She's visibly comforted by his assurance. We spend the rest of the evening dissecting different courses of action—from a direct approach of confronting him with our grievances all the way to a hostile takeover. We look at undermining family confidence in him, enabling us to slide into leadership. We even consider using meds to orchestrate a seemingly natural death. Every possible prerequisite and consequence are examined.

By the time we part for the night, we are all somewhat

overwhelmed and on edge. The non-fatal solutions all require a length of time to enact and can't be guaranteed to succeed. Death guarantees Christiano is removed from power but creates a greater risk of retaliation from his disciples should our hand in his death be uncovered. We would prefer not to create a riff in the family.

While no single plan is agreed upon, several promising options are identified. I can only hope that once the others have time to process our discussion, they will come to the same conclusion as I have. The most logical, efficient answer ends in death.

DINNER AT CHRISTIANO'S Tuxedo Park home a few days later is an utter disaster. He obnoxiously insinuates at every opportunity that a relationship between Ari and I exists when it doesn't. I can feel Luisa's distress in each and every minute that ticks by, but I can do nothing to fix it. My anger simmers dangerously close to the surface by the end of the night. However, I cannot allow him to see how much he upsets me. My anger would undoubtedly trigger his defenses and make action against him more difficult.

Instead, I cage my emotions and paint the perfect mask of indifference on my face. By the time the night is over, I'm exhausted from the effort of my restraint, but I have to push past it. I need to apologize to Isa. She doesn't respond as I expect. Instead, she confronts me, eyes full of tears, and nothing I say can ease her heartache. I don't even know for sure what we plan to do about the matter, but even if I did, I refuse to endanger her by giving her that information.

"Are you going to refuse him or not?" She wants to know if I'll agree to marry Arianna.

The problem with a simple yes or no is that one of the scenarios favored by my cohorts involves Ari and me marrying to ensure I'm promoted to underboss before we carry out Christiano's removal. Without me being positioned in direct succession to the boss, the possibilities become open to other challengers emerging. At that point, any capo could vie for leadership. Should that avenue be taken, I would be lying if I told her I planned to refuse the marriage. I can't tell Isa there is a chance I'll marry Ari and convince her that it will only be a temporary ruse. Not when she's already so upset.

I do my best to assure her that I am handling the matter, but my weak explanation only makes things worse. When she disappears inside her house, heartbroken and resigned, I feel the connection between us pull taut and dangerously thin.

This can't continue. If we don't do something to stop Christiano now, I risk losing Luisa forever. That is simply not an option.

Teeth clenched painfully tight, I get back in the car and return to Hardwick. The sun hasn't even crested over the horizon the next morning when I depart for the city. Too many matters need my attention for me to sleep.

First, I deal with my brother and the clusterfuck of a situation he's created with Livia. Once that is settled, I reach out to Ari and Savio. We gather again that night, safely tucked away at Savio's place. I don't want to chance Christiano seeing either of them come or go from my city apartment. The three of us debate for hours. Ari has finally resigned herself to the conclusion that her father's death is the surest way forward, but she is hesitant to rush any plans. I try to argue that waiting will only make things worse.

I don't hear from Luisa all day. I don't reach out to her either because nothing has changed. I am still unable to make her any promises, and I refuse to lie to her.

One day bleeds into two.

I think about her incessantly. She is my motivation for each of my actions and every word I speak. All I do is in pursuit of a life for us—a way forward.

On the third day, I receive a notification from my alarm system that my house has been entered, which leads me to discover a missed call and text from Luisa. She's gone to my apartment looking for me. I'd like to believe this is simply an attempt to mend a broken fence, but my gut tells me there's more to it. Something's happened in my absence.

I drop what I'm doing and race to my place. When I arrive, I find her asleep on my sofa. She looks regal with her eyes peacefully shut, full lips softly parted. I could watch her sleep for hours, but I need to know what's happened. I'm about to give her shoulder a nudge when her eyes crack open.

"Oh, you're here." She bolts upright, a mix of anxious energy and sleep-mused haze. "I'm sorry to intrude, but I had to talk to you." Her hands attempt to smooth her hair, pulling it back behind her shoulders and exposing a mottled ring of purple blossoming around her neck.

My hand floats of its own volition to the tender markings while stone-cold fury slows my heartbeat until I'm not sure I'm human anymore. Liquid vengeance runs through my veins. I am composed entirely of wrath, a merciless bloodlust.

"Is that bruising around your throat?" I know the answer, but I ask anyway. I can't unleash the beast raging inside me unless absolutely certain it's necessary.

"Christiano came by the cottage this morning," she says softly.

"He did this?"

Isa nods.

She has given me all the confirmation I need. Christiano will die, and he will die at my hands, whether my friends will help me or not. No more debates. No more doubts.

A plan crystalizes in my mind with perfect clarity. I know what we need to do and am anxious to start preparations, but I need to fix things with Luisa first. None of it means anything if she loses faith in me. I spend the rest of the day and night proving my devotion. Apologizing for the past and promising her the future.

When Christiano shows at my apartment the next morning, I give him one final chance to redeem himself and back down from his ridiculous delusion of me marrying Ari. Not only does he not back down but he also makes the final mistake of threatening me. If he thinks he can bully me into a marriage, he truly is deluded. I allow him to leave my apartment without challenge, safe in the knowledge that in less than a week, his reign will be over.

After I take Luisa home to her parents that night, I go straight back to the city. To Arianna's apartment. She's not expecting me, but I luck out and catch her at home.

"What are you doing here?" she asks warily in greeting, keenly aware of the unusual nature of my surprise visit.

"We need to talk. Will you come for a drive?" I wouldn't put it past Christiano to bug his daughter's apartment. I'm not talking about plans to kill him anywhere near his turf.

"Yeah, let me grab my purse."

A few minutes later, we are immersed in evening traffic with no destination in mind.

"What's this all about?" she asks.

"I know you don't want to be pushed into anything, but we don't have any more time to waste, Ari. He went to her house yesterday—choked and threatened her." I glance over and meet her worried gaze in the darkness. "You know as well as I do that he'll kill her. Imagine if that were Grace." I pull the car over into a vacant parking spot along the street.

Ari fidgets uncomfortably in her seat. She didn't realize I knew about her relationship. Hell, she had no idea I knew she liked women. Years ago, when Christiano first started talking about Ari and me marrying, I dug into her background. I wanted to know about the woman being thrust into my life. I'd grown up knowing who she was, but I hadn't spent time with her like Savio had. I didn't truly *know* her.

My investigation unearthed every facet of her life, and thanks to Luisa, I also knew about her newest love interest.

"What do you think will happen if he figures out the truth about you?" Patience thinning, my words are clipped and harsh.

A spark of strength stiffens her spine. "Is that a threat?"

"No, Arianna. I'm only pointing out the reality of your situation. If I can find out, don't you think he will? And then what? You think he won't hesitate to kill whoever you're with as punishment? There isn't a progressive bone in that man's body. He'll never understand."

I let my words hang in the silence. The tinted windows mute the city lights, casting us in darkness.

Eventually, Ari wipes at her eyes and nods. "Okay."

"I need to know you're certain, Arianna. I can't question your commitment to something so dangerous."

"I wouldn't say it if I didn't mean it," she shoots back at me. "It's not his death that scares me. I would be thrilled to be free of him. It's failing that worries me. If it doesn't work. If he survives and learns who betrayed him—" Her body visibly shudders at the thought.

I take her hand in mine and squeeze. "That's not going to happen. I have a plan, and if we all stick together, I know it's going to work."

SAVIO IS on board the minute I tell him my plan. Together, we work through all the kinks so that when the Friday evening engagement dinner rolls around, we are confident and prepared for any number of possible scenarios to unfold.

When Christiano is invited to the party, he's told the event begins an hour later than the actual start. Arianna comes over before him under the pretense of helping me set up, and he's only too happy to think we are finally yielding to his wishes and spending time together.

Ari assures me the security cameras have been turned off before Savio and I slip away to conduct our little office illusion. After a quick change of clothes, I slip out the side of the house and hurry for the street where I left my car for easy access.

The next few minutes happen in a blur.

I do my best to subdue my adrenaline as I walk to Christiano's front door. I know what is about to happen, though it is the most regrettable part of this endeavor. I have no argument with the two soldiers Christiano uses for security, but there is no way around their death. They are always with him and unquestionably loyal. Unfortunately for them, they also trust me not to be a threat.

When I walk in the front door, I wait until both are in quick shot of one another before ending their lives. My remorse is minimal, however, because everything unfolding is Christiano's fault. He has brought about this turn of events by forcing our hands. Others may argue that I chose to pull the trigger, and thus, I'm the only one to blame, but I don't really give a fuck what anyone else thinks. I'm protecting the woman I love, and I will never regret that.

"Well, I have to say, that was unexpected." Christiano

stands near the kitchen without a hint of emotion on his face.

I shouldn't be surprised. What does death mean to a sociopath? Nothing. My betrayal is the only thing that registers with him.

"When you lead by fear, you breed resentment. None of this should come as a shock." I keep my gun trained on him, a silencer over the barrel to ensure no shots are heard. "Though, your ability to incite those closest to you is impressive." I pause for effect, wanting to bask in the moment of his realization that his own flesh and blood rose up against him. "Me—your next-in-command. Your nephew. Your *daughter*."

His eyes narrow and twitch. I've gotten to him, as I knew I would.

"Arianna would *never*," he sneers.

"That's where you're wrong." I glance briefly around the room. "She even turned off the cameras for me."

His upper lip crooks in a snarl. "I never should have let her near that cunt of yours. She's poisoned everything she touched. That little bitch—"

The muffled blast of the gun echoes through the cavernous room before Christiano spins and crashes to the floor behind him. I only engaged in conversation with him to make certain he knew who was responsible for his undoing. He had no right to any last words, and he certainly had no right to spew his venom about Luisa.

I walk to his body and check for a pulse. It's faint but present. I stay crouched next to him and wait until blood no longer pumps through his veins and his body deflates with his final breath. Then I walk away feeling only relief and assurance that we've done the right thing.

Christiano De Bellis can no longer torment us.

Back at my house, I meet with Savio, exchange clothes, then join everyone on the back plaza. I try to keep my earlier demeanor intact, but I only have eyes for Isa. I need to touch her, feel her skin on mine and know deep in my soul that she's safe.

She looks stunning tonight. It had been hard to concentrate on anything but our plan earlier in the evening, but now, Isa is my everything. I can concentrate all my attention on her, as it should be.

"Is everything okay?" she asks, worry creasing her forehead.

I pull her in close and press my lips to the soft skin of her temple. "Everything is just fine," I assure the both of us. And it is because we're together. So long as Luisa is at my side, anything is possible, and I plan to keep her there forever.

With my hand at her back, I direct her into the crowd to meet my associates. The first step in our new lives together. Our night will end in chaos, but for now, I embrace the glimpse of our future. An enduring love. Faith in one another. And loyalty that knows no bounds. A relationship with such solid foundations will see us through any struggle, and for those outside threats beyond our control, there is always the quick solution of a well-aimed bullet. Anything for my Isa.

Thank you so much for reading *Silent Prejudice*! The *Pride and Prejudice* cast of characters is long beloved to so many of us, and I truly hope I did each of them justice.

**Want to check out more of my books?**
Download *Forever Lies*, the first book of The Five Families Series, for free!

Five minutes in a stalled elevator was all it took to turn Alessia Genovese's world upside down. She was just one among millions of New Yorkers, but now, she's landed on Luca Romano's radar, and he isn't about to let her walk away. Dragging her into his world of lies and deceit, Luca's secret agenda shatters Alessia's perfectly crafted life. Sometimes lies are easier than the truth...
*Flip a few more pages to read the first chapter!*

Make sure to join my Facebook reader group and keep in touch!
**Jill's Ravenous Readers**

## Acknowledgments

When I began the journey of transporting Darcy and Elizabeth into a modern-day world of danger and deceit, I knew there was only one place for their story to begin. I was young when I first viewed the magnificent estates at Tuxedo Park, yet I can still remember their impact with such clarity. The gated entry sat beneath a canopy of ancient trees, leading to a winding drive around the lake where homes steeped in history dotted the hillsides. I felt as though I'd passed through a gateway in time rather than a security checkpoint.

I'd like to thank a dear family friend, Peter Regna, for providing me the opportunity for such creative inspiration. Everything about Tuxedo Park was perfect. The exterior Spanish accents of his estate were used to craft my vision of Christiano's mansion, while memories of the interior became the historic halls of Hardwick. Peter couldn't have possibly known a simple visit would make such an impact, but it did. And I think it's a beautiful reminder of how we are all capable of making a positive mark on others' lives with the simplest of gestures.

# ABOUT THE AUTHOR

Jill Ramsower is a life-long Texan—born in Houston, raised in Austin, and currently residing in West Texas. She attended Baylor University and subsequently Baylor Law School to obtain her BA and JD degrees. She spent the next fourteen years practicing law and raising her three children until one fateful day, she strayed from the well-trod path she had been walking and sat down to write a book. An addict with a pen, she set to writing like a woman possessed and discovered that telling stories is her passion in life.

# SOCIAL MEDIA & WEBSITE

**Release Day Alerts, Sneak Peak, and Newsletter**
To be the first to know about upcoming releases, please join Jill's Newsletter. (No spam or frequent pointless emails.)
**Jill's Newsletter**

Official Website: www.jillramsower.com
Jill's Facebook Page: www.facebook.com/jillramsowerauthor
Reader Group: Jill's Ravenous Readers
Follow Jill on Instagram: @jillramsowerauthor
Follow Jill on Twitter: @JRamsower

Interested in reading the book that kicked off *The Five Families Series*? Check out the book readers are calling "one bombshell after another."

**Forever Lies**
By
**Jill Ramsower**

Here's a taste of Alessia and Luca's gripping tale ...

# CHAPTER 1
*Alessia*

The sight of the silver elevator doors closing before I could reach them caused my chest to clamp tight with desperation.

"Hold the doors, *please!*" I called out over the clatter of my stilettos on the marble floor.

Hiding from my boss would be so much harder if I didn't get my ass tucked away in my office before he arrived. If he'd simply been the overly chatty sort or socially awkward, I wouldn't bother with my elaborate evasion schemes, but it was so much worse than that. I would do whatever I could to avoid spending a single unnecessary minute with that man.

If I missed this elevator, would I be forced to ride the next one with my boss? He'd be arriving at the building any minute. Ten floors, alone, in an enclosed space with the creep.

My heart seized painfully.

A second before the doors could seal shut, they froze with a jerk, then retracted, allowing me to scramble aboard.

"Thank you so much. You really don't understand—" My words trailed away when my eyes landed on the man who had saved me from potential misery.

He was masculine beauty personified—dark hair, perfectly styled back and closely cropped on the sides. He had a dusting of dark hair on his angular jaw, and his deep-set eyes were so dark that they were almost black. Without saying a word, easy confidence wafted from his expensively suited form like steam from a rain-soaked summer street.

I had never seen him before. I'd come to recognize many of the building's occupants, but there was no chance I would have forgotten the sight of him.

He was the most breathtaking man I'd ever seen.

Towering over me, despite my four-inch heels, he owned every square inch of the small elevator car. While he was only a few years older than me, he had the powerful presence of a much older man.

"What don't I understand?" The amused purr of his voice was a warm caress that stole the air from my lungs.

Fortunately, the elevator doors closing behind me jarred me from my trance, reminding me I'd been unabashedly devouring him with my eyes. I exhaled a shaky breath as I turned and pushed the button for the tenth floor.

"Just that I needed to get upstairs. Don't want to be late for work." I forced an awkward chuckle, looking anywhere but at the gorgeous man directly across from me until I realized I could feel the penetrating touch of his eyes. I didn't have to look up to know he was staring at me, daring me to meet his gaze. Unable to ignore his unspoken command, I lifted my eyes and peered at him through my lashes.

When my gaze reached his face, one corner of his mouth quirked up just a fraction. Had I not been so keenly aware of the man, I would have missed the fleeting movement. Leaning back against the wall, hands clasped casually in front of him, he was perfectly at ease, amused by my flustered reaction.

I, on the other hand, was coming apart under his scrutiny.

Why was I so affected by a man I'd never even met? He was nobody to me. What did I care what he thought of me? There were loads of attractive men in the city.

*This man is different.*

His commanding stare stripped my defenses and left me raw and vulnerable.

Just when I thought I would blurt something to fill the uncomfortable silence, the elevator shuddered, then ground to a stop, lights flickering. My hand darted out to catch myself against the wall, and I gasped in surprise. The man, on the other hand, needed no such balance assistance. Aside from a glance around the elevator car, he was seemingly unfazed.

Why should the laws of physics affect someone so clearly not of this world?

"Looks like we're stuck," I murmured after it became clear the doors were not opening, nor were we resuming motion. "I suppose we should call for help." I glanced down at the phone labeled for emergency use on my side of the elevator, and when I looked back up, the man's piercing gaze was still fixed on me.

He pulled away from the wall and closed the space between us, making my breath catch in my throat. Leaning across me, just inches from touching me, he opened the call box and retrieved the phone. I released a shaky exhale and took a small step back to give him room and to collect myself.

"Yes, my companion and I are stuck in one of the elevators in the Triton building ... No emergencies, just stuck ... Thank you." He hung up the receiver and turned to where I now stood in the back corner, having inched away from him as he spoke. "They've sent someone to check on the situation, but there's no telling how long it will be." His deep voice resonated throughout the small space, each syllable oozing control. The sound was the perfect complement to his unflappable demeanor.

My heart pounded so fast, I became lightheaded. I'd been around assertive men all my life, but this man's presence filled up the small space so completely, there was no oxygen left to breathe. My eyes flitted to his, and I offered him a glimpse of a smile. "It's not the first time I've been stuck in an elevator. Live in the city long enough, and you come to expect these things." Relief coursed through my veins when I managed to utter something semi-intelligible.

"You work in the building?" Leaning his shoulder against the side wall, he continued to focus all his attention on me, not returning to his side of the elevator.

"Yes, I work at Triton. You?"

"No, I'm here to meet someone."

He stared at me for a long moment. It felt as though he was measuring my worth, as if he could see deep inside of me and was perusing my most personal thoughts.

The tension in the small space was more than palpable—it was a physical force pressing against my skin.

"Luca," he rumbled as he extended his hand, finally breaking the silence.

He was introducing himself. What did that mean? Was he merely being polite in an awkward situation, or was he taking the opportunity to hit on me?

"Alessia."

His hand was rough but warm, and he held my much smaller hand for longer than was necessary.

*Hitting on me. Okay, Alessia. You can do this. Play it cool.*

As he released my fingers, his thumb stroked along the back of my hand, sending tingles across my skin, cascading up my arm and down into the pit of my belly.

"That's Italian, right?"

"Yes," I breathed. "You as well?"

"I am." His head angled to the side. "Are you seeing anyone Alessia?"

My eyes danced from one shiny metal wall to the other. Was this really happening? Was this god-like man asking me out while we were trapped in an elevator together? Had I hit my head and dreamed this entire situation while comatose in a hospital bed? It seemed too fantastical to be real, but I had no other explanation.

*Answer the man, Les. Before he thinks you're crazy.*

"Um, no. No, I'm not."

The first hint of a smile formed on his perfect lips, but before he could respond, the elevator lurched back into motion.

Luca reached forward and pressed the stop button, and the elevator ground to a jarring halt again.

My brows creased in confusion.

"Give me your phone," he ordered softly, palm outstretched.

Common sense should have screamed at me not to turn over my sole source of communication while this man had me trapped with him, but I'd apparently woken up low on all forms of self-preservation. Something about his commanding tone spoke to deep-seated need within me to comply.

Eyes wide, like a lamb to the slaughter, I placed my phone in his hand.

He arched a brow. "Unlock it, Alessia."

My name on his tongue was the sweetest nectar I could have imagined—delicious, tempting, and dangerously addictive. The slightest twinge of fear pricked at the back of my neck. Somewhere deep down, I sensed this man had the potential to undo me—take me in, rearrange my insides, and spit me back out after I was unrecognizable.

I chided myself for overreacting. This was a five-minute conversation with a man in an elevator, not an arranged marriage. I needed to get a grip on myself. As soon as he pressed the button again, we would be on our way, and I would likely never see him again.

He tapped at my phone before a buzzing sounded in his breast pocket. He pulled out his own device and began to type, my phone still firmly cradled in his other hand. "I'd like to hear more about you and your family, but it looks like our ride is almost over, so we'll have to continue the conversation another time."

He closed the space between us, and instead of handing back my phone, he reached over and slid the device back inside my purse, bringing us within inches of one another. Heat radiated off him, tugging at me to close the gap and press my body against his. My eyes leapt up to his, my mouth softly parted as I struggled to keep my wits.

"It was a pleasure meeting you," he rasped before stepping back and pressing the button behind him without severing our connection. "I'll be in touch." The moment the doors opened, he was gone.

*Holy fuck, what just happened?*

It was like a scene from a movie—that crap didn't happen in real life. Yes, I was an attractive woman, but that usually meant I got cat-calls from construction workers and hit on by slimy douchebags. Rarely was the attention wanted, and the feelings were almost never reciprocated on my end.

I only had a matter of seconds to gather my thoughts and collect myself before the elevator doors opened onto my floor. With uneven steps, I entered the Triton lobby, a bemused grin plastered on my face.

*What a surreal start to my day!*

Thoughts of Luca were almost distracting enough to make me forget about my lecherous boss.

Almost.

Each step I took closer toward our adjoining offices brought back a renewed sense of doom. Not to mention a healthy dose of anger.

Roger Coleman was the smarmiest, most disgusting man I'd ever met, but he was also damn good at hiding his true nature. He'd held his position at Triton Construction for well over a decade and was an established member of the good 'ol boys club. A brotherhood of men led by the owner of the company—a man who also happened to be my father.

Dad had built Triton into the largest construction company in New York with a lifetime of dedication and a ruthless mind for business. Triton was his pride and joy, and I desperately wanted to join him at the helm of his company. More than anything, I wanted to make my father proud, and I wouldn't accomplish that by running to him every time I had a problem. I needed to handle Roger on my own. He was just a misogynic sleaze, after all. If I could grow a spine and be firm with him, he wouldn't be an issue.

Admittedly, I'd done an abysmal job so far.

I wasn't the best at handling conflict, and he always seemed to catch me off guard. No matter how many scenarios I rehearsed in my head, his veiled innuendo and unsettling looks left me speechless. I'd heard of fight or flight, but my default setting was most definitely to freeze, and overcoming that instinct had proven more challenging than I'd hoped.

Roger's advances had started out small—telling me how lovely I looked or commenting on my hair or eyes. In romance novels, having an older executive pursue the young professional sounded sexy and exciting, but when my fifty-five-year-old boss with a fake-and-bake tan and leathery skin started hitting on me, it was repulsive and unsettling. I'd done my best to discretely brush aside his advances and discourage his behavior in the hopes he would take the hint and move on, but after a year of working in the office, he had yet to cease his efforts.

Only once had his pursuit escalated to a physical level. Six months ago, at the company Christmas party he cornered me in a hallway and pressed me against a wall, his dick thrust against my stomach. He'd been drinking heavily, and I made the mistake of walking to a restroom alone. I'd been so repulsed and terrified, I didn't even hear the unquestionably revolting comment he made. I gave a stuttered excuse and tore from his grasp, leaving the party without another word.

The incident had been seared into my brain. I tried to tell myself it was an isolated incident that wouldn't have happened had alcohol not been present, but I couldn't shake the lingering anxiety that he'd try again. I took every effort to distance myself from the man, both professionally and physically. I made certain I pulled in coworkers to help on projects, so there was always an extra set of eyes working with us.

Our offices, along with several others in the suite, were constructed with glass walls, which helped give me a certain degree of security—no hiding behind closed doors outside of the conference or break room. Another fortifying fact—Roger's advances weren't a daily affair, not even weekly. The problem wasn't their frequency; it was the uncertainty of not knowing when they might occur that was the most stressful.

This week I was in for a treat. Today was the only day I'd have to deal with Roger before he left on a week-long business trip to L.A.

I could survive one day with the devil.

Most of the morning passed uneventfully. I was left to my own devices, preparing for a full week of project meetings and impending deadlines. It wasn't until almost eleven when the intercom on my phone blared with Roger's voice.

"Alessia, can you come in here, please?"

A seemingly harmless request, but it stirred an overwhelming sense of dread in the pit of my stomach.

I didn't answer—there was no need. He could see me as I stood from my chair and made my way to his office next door. While I didn't so much as glance his direction, I had no doubt his beady eyes would follow my every step. Our offices lined the outer wall of windows—the glass walls allowing the rest of the employees to enjoy the soaring views from our building. It was a double-edged sword—no privacy was a good thing, but it also meant there was no escaping Roger's stare.

"Did you need something?" I stopped several feet from his small conference table where he'd laid out his presentation materials.

"You sure you can't come with me? You know the material as well as I do and would be an enormous help when I make the pitch. It's not too late to get you a ticket." He arched a brow, hands propped on his hips where he stood on the opposite side of the table.

"My sisters would kill me if I'm not there to help get ready for Mom's party this weekend. It's her fiftieth and—"

"I know, I know," he cut me off as I began to blather about my mother's pretend birthday. She'd turned fifty years ago, but the party had been the best excuse I'd come up with on the spot when Roger had initially asked me to accompany him on the trip. There was no way in hell I was traveling with the man. Fortunately, he hadn't bothered verifying my story, so I continued to uphold the ruse.

"You told me already. Well, get over here and let's run through everything one more time before I head to the airport." He waved me over with a frown, clearly disgruntled I hadn't caved to his pressure to accompany him.

The project was a relatively minor remodel proposal for a building in Brooklyn owned by a corporation headquartered on the opposite coast. I'd worked on the project along with a couple other people from our team. It was too small-scale for Roger to do the grunt work, but he was presenting our proposal because the contact was a friend of his. We had already given him all the pertinent information on multiple occasions, so I wasn't sure what I was supposed to say.

The chairs had been pulled around to clump on my side of the table with the various documents and exhibits spread out for viewing from the other side. His setup left little option except to come around to his side of the table, but I kept as much distance between us as was reasonably possible.

"It looks like everything is here," I offered as I perused the materials.

"What about the schedule of work?" he asked as he leaned forward to retrieve the document. "I noticed we listed a completion timeframe of six months, but I thought we had discussed moving that out to nine." His right hand snaked out to curl around my waist and pull me next to him while his other hand held out the document as if showing me its contents was the purpose behind his flagrant violation of my personal space.

Stunned by his action, I took the papers and stared at them dumbly. I didn't see the words on the page—I was entirely focused inside my head where my thoughts raced at a frenzied pace in an attempt to grasp my situation. My boss's hand lingered at my lower back, the insidious warmth seeping into my skin, before slowly dropping down to caress over the curve of my ass cheek.

I ceased breathing, and my ears began to ring.

His repulsive touch in such a private area made my skin crawl, but I couldn't seem to move a muscle.

I was frozen—horror battling with mortification.

The glass walls gave me a perfect view of the bustling office where a dozen employees scurried about their business. Never in a thousand years had I imagined he would make a move on me in plain sight of our coworkers, but he'd done a masterful job keeping his actions unseen. To all the world, we looked as though we were simply examining a document—his wandering hand only visible to the New York skyline out our tenth-floor windows.

"Um ... we decided ... to subcontract the welding work," I sputtered out. "Our guys will be busy on the Merchant project. Outsourcing will enable us to keep the six-month timeline the client requested." As I said the words, I frantically debated what to do. If I allowed him to continue touching me, it would no doubt encourage the asshole to take more liberties. If I confronted him or in any way made a scene, the entire office would know in seconds. Before I had a chance to decide, the intercom in his office crackled to life.

"Mr. Coleman, your flight leaves in two hours."

The instant his assistant, Beverly, began to speak, I pulled out of his grasp and fled the office. Bypassing my own office, I hurried to the restrooms and locked myself in a stall. Leaning against the door, head back and eyes closed, I tried to regulate my erratic heartrate.

*Did that really just happen?*

Could I have imagined the whole thing? Surely, my boss hadn't assaulted me in front of the entire office. As much as I wished it had been a nightmare, it wasn't. Each agonizing second had played out in living color, and I had stood immobile like a squirrel starring down an approaching car. What was wrong with me? Why hadn't I pulled away instantly? Why hadn't I swallowed my pride and told my father the truth months ago or just turned Roger's balding ass into HR? I'd had my reasons at the time, but they seemed less and less valid with each new day. My conflict and self-doubt brought on a barrage of guilt and blame that bowed my shoulders with their oppressive weight.

I needed to get out of the building.

I exited the stall and went through the motions of washing my hands before walking to my office with my eyes lowered to the geometric patterns of the grey commercial carpeting. Grabbing my phone, I texted my cousin to move up our lunch date, then snagged my purse and scurried out of my office. Normally, I would inform a coworker if I was leaving early, but I couldn't do it. I felt exposed—like anyone who looked at me would know what I had allowed to happen. I couldn't force myself to take that chance—to let them see the shame in my eyes. Instead, I kept my head down and hurried out the closest exit.

I couldn't allow my boss's behavior to continue.

The realization was daunting.

Now, I just had to figure out what I was going to do about it. Would I confront Roger myself? Would I file a complaint with HR or go straight to my father? If I told my dad, would he believe me or think I was overreacting? Roger was his friend, after all. And if Roger wasn't immediately fired, would he know I'd reported him? How would a man with such little moral character respond when he found out I'd put his job in jeopardy?

The possibilities paralyzed me.

*You have the rest of the week to figure it out, Les. Try not to panic.*

I wasn't normally the type to procrastinate, but in this case, I needed time to process. I needed to talk through everything and make sure I took the proper steps, because once I started that ball rolling, there would be no stopping it.

Fortunately for me, I already had lunch scheduled with my cousin, Giada. She would be the perfect sounding board. Until then, I would ignore all thoughts of Roger to protect my sanity. I shoved the incident into a dark corner of my mind—somewhere next to the misery of my first period and getting lost as a child in the subway—and prayed my dramatic morning had no more surprises in store for me.

Want to read more?
Get Forever Lies HERE!

www.ingramcontent.com/pod-product-compliance
Lightning Source LLC
Chambersburg PA
CBHW032336250725
30185CB00009B/292